LUCY JANE

Also by
Susan Hampshire

LUCY JANE
AT THE
BALLET

To all children who are in hospital

The author is sharing her royalties with
Tadworth Court Hospital, which
provides treatment and care for
chronically sick and handicapped
children.

Susan Hampshire

LUCY JANE
ON
TELEVISION

Illustrated by Vanessa Julian-Ottie

METHUEN CHILDREN'S BOOKS

*My grateful thanks to Vanessa Julian-Ottie
for her vivid drawings which bring Lucy Jane
to life so beautifully. To Kerry Jane and Pierre
Vacher who let me use their son's room in
Barbados to finish the second draft. To the
staff of the Alpenkrone Hotel, Filtzmoos,
Austria, for their understanding and kindness
as I locked myself in my room for days at a time
to finish the book. I would also like to thank
my cousin Angela, who inspired one of the
characters.*

*Many thanks, too, to Janine Fischer,
Maureen Defries and Sheila Hoad for so
patiently typing all the different versions of
the book.*

*And most important of all, a million thanks to
Miriam Hodgson, for whose faith and tireless
guidance I am extremely grateful. And last,
but not least, to my husband Eddie for his
continued interest in Lucy Jane.*

First published in 1989
by Methuen Children's Books,
A Division of the Octopus Group Ltd,
Michelin House, 81 Fulham Road,
London SW3 6RB.
Text copyright © Susan Hampshire 1989
Illustrations copyright © Vanessa Julian-Ottie 1989
Printed in Great Britain
by St Edmundsbury Press, Bury St Edmunds, Suffolk

British Library Cataloguing in Publication Data

Hampshire, Susan, *1942-*
Lucy Jane on television.
I Title II Julian-Ottie, Vanessa
823'.914 [J]

ISBN 0–416–14922–7

O416 149 227 5573

Contents

1

The Surprise

When Lucy Jane Tadworth was nine and her mother was in hospital having Jeremy, Lucy Jane went to stay with her aunt, who was the wardrobe mistress for the ballet at Covent Garden. There, quite unexpectedly, Lucy Jane appeared in the Christmas Gala performance of the *Nutcracker* ballet and danced in front of the Royal Family. It was so exciting that ever since Lucy Jane had been hoping that something as wonderful would happen again. But Lucy Jane hadn't seen her aunt as she'd been working in America. Lucy Jane hadn't even been to the ballet from that exciting Christmas holiday to this warm summer when her parents decided that she should take her first aeroplane trip alone to visit her grandmother in Scotland.

Lucy Jane wasn't at all happy about the idea; she was certain she would miss Jeremy, and her cat Tilly. She hated the thought of being away from her parents and she knew there would be no friends for her to play with as her grandmother didn't seem to know any children of Lucy Jane's age.

But Lucy Jane was not a child to make a fuss and only said to her mother, 'Going to Scotland without everyone is like ice-cream without jelly. That is,' she added quickly, 'if you really like jelly.'

Her mother smiled. She realized that Lucy Jane was not keen on going to Scotland but everything had already been arranged so she just answered kindly, 'Granny says it will put roses in your cheeks.'

'I don't want to look like Aunt Sally in Worzle Gummidge!' Lucy Jane laughed, then made a face.

'Enough of that!' her mother answered and handed Lucy Jane the knives and forks for her to help lay the table for lunch.

On the day that Lucy Jane was to leave she felt extremely sad to say goodbye to her home. She loved it. It was pretty and brightly furnished, often untidy and filled with so much laughter, especially from Lucy Jane's mother.

During the drive to the airport Lucy Jane, who was rather proud of being known as a 'chatterbox', was very silent. Although Mrs Skipp, who helped with the cleaning on Saturdays, promised to look after Tilly, Lucy Jane was sure that the cat would miss her.

'If Tilly doesn't eat while I'm away you'd better call the doctor,' Lucy Jane remarked seriously.

'The vet,' her mother corrected her, 'or I could look after her – after all, I am a doctor!'

'Get set vet to grasshopper to pet,' Lucy Jane commented as she sat clutching her Snoopy lunch box filled with treats for the journey, the pink plastic purse, a present from her best friend Julie, and five pounds her father had given her in case of emergencies. She wished with all her heart that the car would break down or run out of petrol so that she would miss the plane. But they arrived at the airport in plenty of time. Lucy Jane's heart sank as her mother heaved her suitcase from the boot of the car.

'I'm worried about the cat,' Lucy Jane suddenly blurted out, anxious to talk without letting her mother know she was still feeling apprehensive about going to Scotland, and nervous of taking the plane on her own, but they walked from the car park to the departure hall in silence.

The departure hall was an enormous, noisy place with hundreds of passengers pushing steel trolleys laden with luggage in every direction and sometimes bumping into each other.

'Just as well mothers don't push their babies in prams around like that,' Lucy Jane remarked as they arrived at the check-in counter, 'otherwise there'd be broken babies all over the place.'

'Just as well,' her mother agreed, as she handed over Lucy Jane's suitcase and ticket.

The air hostess looked at Lucy Jane. 'Is this little girl travelling alone?'

'Yes,' Lucy Jane answered immediately. 'I've *got* to go to see my granny for five whole weeks and I expect I shall be more bored than a bumble bee,' she announced, trying to hide her fear of leaving her parents and brother behind.

The lady behind the counter came round and placed a plastic envelope on a string round Lucy Jane's neck. It had large initials U.M. marked on it and inside there was Lucy Jane's ticket.

'U.M.! Those aren't my initials,' Lucy Jane said, looking at the plastic holder.

'It means "Unaccompanied Minor", ' the air hostess said kindly. 'That's what you are today, as you're travelling alone.'

'I wish I wasn't,' Lucy Jane thought, now feeling quite sick at the idea.

'You'd better say goodbye to your mother now,' the hostess suggested. 'I have to take you to board your flight.'

A sharp pricking sensation immediately began at the back of Lucy Jane's eyes, and a lump formed in her throat. She didn't want to look at her mother in case her mother noticed that she was about to cry. For the first time Lucy Jane was grateful that she had started to wear glasses.

'I don't see why I should have to spend five whole weeks with Granny,' she whispered softly as her mother put her arm around her shoulder. 'I'm sure Jeremy will miss me and . . . ' She didn't manage to finish her sentence.

Tears were rolling down Lucy Jane's cheeks; she was feeling very sorry for herself and too proud to kiss her mother goodbye. Her glasses fogged up and it was hard to see. But her mother hugged and kissed her again and Lucy Jane was glad. But instead of kissing her mother goodbye, she clutched her belongings to her chest and said, 'I'm going to hate the whole holiday, every single sixty seconds of each minute, each sixty minutes of each hour, each twenty-four hours of each day!'

Mrs Tadworth laughed. 'Heavens, Lucy, what a mouthful. I'm sure once you arrive in Scotland you'll find lots of good surprises awaiting you.'

'I'll find Granny awaiting me,' Lucy Jane replied

seriously, and with that she kissed her mother, gave her a big hug and walked, chin in the air, with the air hostess to the plane.

To Lucy Jane's delight she discovered that travelling on her own was a great treat. The stewardesses made a real fuss of her and she was given two extra sweets before the plane took off, plus three comic books, a puzzle and some crayons.

'Excuse me,' Lucy Jane asked the air hostess anxiously as she walked down the narrow space between the seats on the plane after the plane had taken off. 'If someone wanted to go to the lavatory while they were on a plane, would they have to wait until they got home?'

'No, there is a toilet on the plane. Would you like to use it?' she said, putting out her hand to the little girl.

'Well,' Lucy Jane smiled, 'yes, please. Just to see that they've really got one,' and she undid her seatbelt and followed the air hostess nervously down the plane to the loo. The rows of seats on either side of the aisle were higher than Lucy Jane's head, with people sitting and reading, talking or sleeping. Lucy Jane noticed that two of the sleeping passengers' heads had drooped to one side, their mouths had fallen open and they were snoring very loudly. She longed to pop one of her boiled sweets into their mouths. Suddenly she stopped.

'Will I need my life jacket?' she asked, alarmed. 'The lady said it was under the seat.'

'No, no,' the hostess replied, smiling.

'This is not a lavatory!' Lucy Jane remarked when she arrived at the entrance door. 'This is a cupboard. I'd like to see the lavatory, please.'

'This is the lavatory,' the hostess said patiently. 'They have to be very small on planes as there's so little space.'

'Lucky I'm not as fat as Mr Peter, our butcher,' Lucy Jane commented as she squeezed in and tried to close the folding door. There was hardly enough room for her to stand. 'Hope Daddy doesn't want to go to the lavatory on a plane,' she thought. After much twisting and turning to lift her skirt, then wash her hands, she emerged from the 'cupboard' feeling pleased that she'd managed so well and returned to her seat.

'Are we still in the sky?' Lucy Jane asked the lady next to her as she settled in her seat. 'We won't fall, will we?' she continued before the lady could reply.

She wondered if the plane had flown over her house and if Jeremy had known she was in the sky, or if any of the water from the wash basin had fallen on to the houses below. She settled into her seat to read her comic.

Suddenly there was an announcement.

'Please fasten your seatbelts for landing,' the Captain's soothing voice called over the loudspeaker.

'Are we there already?' a surprised Lucy Jane asked the hostess, who was checking that Lucy Jane's seatbelt was safely fastened and that her seat was upright.

'Yes, we'll touch down in a moment and then I'll escort you to the party who is meeting you at the airport.'

'It's not a party,' Lucy Jane answered seriously. 'It's just my granny, Mrs Mackenzie.'

The hostess nodded. 'That's what I meant.' She took her own seat ready for the aeroplane's landing.

Waiting for Lucy Jane at the barrier was Lucy Jane's grandmother. She was a stout, cuddly-looking woman with short, curly grey hair, silver-rimmed glasses and a smiling face. Her cheeks were rather pink, the way she wanted Lucy Jane's to be! Lucy Jane liked her grandmother, and although she was afraid of her sometimes, she knew she was only thinking of what was best for her when she said things like, 'Eat up all your cabbage,' or 'Now run along into the garden and get some fresh air.'

Her grandmother stood beaming at the barrier, and when Lucy Jane saw her she had a sudden feeling of happiness and she skipped towards her saying, 'I didn't get any feathers in my tummy, or birds in my feet, on the plane. I ate sweets and washed my hands all over London.'

Her grandmother laughed. 'Hello, darling,' she smiled as Lucy Jane and the air hostess came towards her. 'Just as I thought, looking peaky. Never mind, I like your glasses. Get your luggage and we'll have some roses in those cheeks in no time.'

'Not unless you put some rouge on them like Aunt Sally,' Lucy Jane replied. 'My skin is always very pale so I doubt I'll ever look "rosy" or whatever you like to call it,' she said, smiling up at her grandmother. She held her grandmother's hand obediently and waited for her case to arrive along the dark, shiny, snake-like conveyor belt. Lucy Jane quickly tried to grab her case but it moved away before she could get it. 'This snake thing doesn't wait for anyone. Don't think we'll ever get my case, Granny.'

'Yes, we will, dearie. Here it is.'

It was an hour from Glasgow airport to her grandmother's house at Rockleigh in the Lowlands, so Mrs Mackenzie had packed up a snack of egg sandwiches, a packet of crisps and a bottle of Lucozade for Lucy Jane to eat in the car.

As Lucy Jane munched away she noticed the local newspaper lying on the back seat beside her. The headline read:

'THE RUSSELL ADVENTURE FILM TO BE MADE FOR TELEVISION IN ROCKLEIGH.'

Then below: *'The Search for Child Star Continues.'*

Lucy Jane looked at the paper more closely, then wiped her glasses on her cardigan and read it again. She looked up and asked her grandmother excitedly, 'Are they making a television film in Scotland, Granny?'

'Yes,' her grandmother answered. 'I thought your mother had told you. A T V company's filming at Rockleigh Castle on the hill, less than a mile from the house.'

'Only a mile from your farmhouse, Granny?' Lucy Jane exclaimed, her head swimming with excitement.

'Yes, but they don't seem to be having any luck finding the right child to star in it,' she replied matter-of-factly.

'Are they looking for a girl or a boy?' Lucy Jane asked eagerly and looked at the newspaper again: *'Auditions are being held at Rockleigh Village School Hall on Monday. The search for girls to test for the television epic continues.'* She was about to finish reading but didn't have time as Mrs Mackenzie announced, 'We're home, Lucy darling,' as they drove up the apple-tree-lined drive to the farmhouse.

'Already?' Lucy Jane asked, surprised, taking off her glasses.

'Yes, pick up your things, give me the paper and come inside to say hello to Mrs Tamm,' said Mrs Mackenzie as she got out of the car.

Lucy Jane quickly gathered up her things and rushed into the house, shouting, 'Hello, Tammy, I'm here!' Mrs Tamm, the housekeeper, came bustling from the kitchen, wiping her hands on her flowered overall to

9

greet her.

'My, Lucy, how you've grown!' she exclaimed as the child danced around her. 'Been in the ballet, too, I hear. My! My!' she exclaimed again, putting the palms of her hands together in a gesture of amazement. Then she gave Lucy Jane a kiss.

'Still got my koala bear?' Lucy Jane asked excitedly.

'Ooh, yes.'

'And the glass animals, are they all safe?' she added quickly.

'Yes, yes, you don't forget a thing, do you?' said Mrs Tamm, pleased to welcome her. She knew Lucy would brighten up Mrs Mackenzie's house and life, and doubtless her own.

'I'll get the tea,' she said. '*And* your favourite cake,' she added as she hurried away laughing, her tall, slim body loping like a giraffe as she made her way to the kitchen.

'Ooh, lovely,' Lucy Jane said, rubbing her hands together at the thought of the chocolate smartie cake, and skipped into the sitting room.

Her grandmother's house was a comfortable, welcoming farmhouse. The surrounding hills and mountains were covered with heather and sheep, with rivers and streams flowing in the valleys between the hills for as far as the eye could see. There were no factories, buildings or lorries. The little village of Rockleigh, half a mile from the farmhouse, was made up of six shops, two inns, a school and a church.

Mrs Mackenzie's sitting room was very simple and comfortable. The squashy armchairs had faded floral linen covers and there were vases of flowers and white china figures standing on all the well-polished furniture. The walls were pale green and the carpet a mushroom colour, and in front of the hearth was a woolly rug that the cat loved to lie on.

The cushions on the chairs were in need of being puffed up and there was a large pile of newspapers on the footstool in front of the sofa. Books were piled in heaps on every available space, most of them with leather book-markers sticking out.

As Lucy Jane looked around the room she felt pleased to be back in Rockleigh, especially because of the film. She wriggled back on to the big sofa, her legs dangling, while Mrs Mackenzie settled in her favourite armchair to pour the tea.

'What do you know about the television, Granny?'

she asked. She had always loved the old-fashioned serials like *The Secret Garden*, and also the funny jokes in *The Cosby Show*.

'Oh, it's some nonsense,' Mrs Mackenzie replied as she sipped her tea. 'Of no interest at all,' she continued. 'These things ruin the countryside and village life and are totally disruptive. The sooner it's over, the better.'

Lucy Jane didn't agree. But she thought it best to keep her curiosity to herself and slowly drank her milky tea in silence, waiting for Mrs Tamm to bring her favourite chocolate smartie cake.

2

Lucy Jane Finds Out More

That night, as Lucy Jane lay in the small whitewashed bedroom next to her grandmother's, she found it hard to sleep. She kept thinking about the audition. She had to try but how would she manage to get there?

She held her 'tickly rug' up to her face and cuddled Mrs Tamm's koala bear and watched the curtains flutter in the open window. It was not dark outside so she knew her grandmother would not have gone to bed yet. But as soon as Lucy Jane heard her grandmother's steps on the stairs and her bedroom door close, she crept from her bed and made her way as quietly as she could downstairs to look for the newspaper.

The sitting room was very dark, and the light of the moon streaming through the window made the room look rather eerie. Lucy Jane found it difficult to make her way round the room without bumping into the furniture. So she screwed up her eyes and stood still for a moment trying to get her bearings when suddenly she caught sight of what she thought was the newspaper lying on the sofa. She made her way towards it, but as she did so she tripped over the footstool, which knocked over a little coffee table at the side of the sofa. There was an enormous crash as the table and the bowl of flowers and a pile of books fell to the floor. Immediately Mrs Tamm's dog started to bark in the kitchen.

'Rats,' Lucy Jane said as she did her best to find her way out of the room. 'And rabbits,' she added as she bumped into the rocking chair on the way to the door.

The dog continued barking. Lucy Jane was so frightened she thought she could see Mrs Tamm glaring at her from the far side of the room, but eventually the dog was quiet and the house silent once more. She tried again and was about to pick up the paper when she heard her grandmother coming out of her bedroom. 'Kitty Boy, I think I heard someone banging about downstairs and the dog was barking,' she said to the cat and made her way downstairs.

Lucy Jane flattened herself against the wall, terrified her grandmother would find her. But luckily Mrs Mackenzie walked straight past her, and Lucy Jane was able to dart from the room and scamper upstairs again before Mrs Mackenzie had time to turn on the light. Just as Lucy Jane slipped into her bedroom she heard her grandmother exclaim, 'Great Heavens!'

It seemed ages before Mrs Mackenzie came back upstairs. Once the coast was clear Lucy Jane tried again. As she walked into the sitting room she felt something brush past her leg. She stood stock-still, not knowing what it was when, suddenly, something touched her leg again.

Lucy Jane was terrified. Then she heard a plaintive 'miaow'. She looked down and there at her feet was Kitty Boy, weaving around her legs. She smiled to think that she had been so easily frightened. Without wasting a moment, she grabbed the paper and tucked it under her nightie and crept upstairs to her room. She quietly closed the door, turned on her bedside light and excitedly settled down to read.

The auditions were to be held on Monday. 'Monday – in three days I must be there,' she thought. Her head suddenly felt as if it was filled with frogs jumping about in excitement. Maybe she would be like Keshia Knight Pulleam, her favourite television actress who played Rudi in *The Cosby Show*, and make everyone laugh.

She snuggled down beneath the covers, drew her knees up to her chest, kissed the koala on the nose, and tried to sleep. She hoped and hoped this holiday would be as exciting as her Christmas ballet holiday. The thought made her curl up her toes. 'I've got mice in my feet I'm so excited,' she said, wishing her mother was there to give her a cuddle. It would be a shame to have another adventure without her.

The next morning was Friday and Mrs Mackenzie drove Lucy Jane into the village. To her grandmother's amazement the sleepy village of Rockleigh was buzzing with activity, with members of the television film crew milling along every street and alley. Big trucks filled with lighting equipment and cameras were parked on the hillside near the great stone castle. Caravans marked 'Make-up and Hairdressing – Artists Only', 'Wardrobe' and 'Children' were lined up in a row on the drive leading up to the castle.

'My word, Lucy,' her grandmother said, as they went

into the newsagent to collect her newspaper and copy of *Scottish Life* magazine. 'The whole village has changed overnight. It must be this awful television thing. How inconvenient.'

'Not inconvenient to me, Granny,' Lucy Jane said happily.

As Lucy Jane did up the button of her cardigan she noticed a large poster in the shop window saying:

'GIRLS BETWEEN 8 AND 11 NEEDED FOR TELEVISION FILM.'

'That's me!' Lucy Jane thought. 'That's me! I'm going to try and be on television.'

'Look, Granny,' Lucy Jane said, jumping up and down. 'Look at that poster.'

'Oh, they're everywhere,' a young voice with a strong Scottish accent said from under the counter. 'They're making such a song and dance the whole village has gone television crazy,' said a cheeky girl with freckles as she came up from under the counter. She was the newsagent's daughter.

'Morning, Mrs M.,' she said brightly to Lucy Jane's grandmother.

'Oh, good morning, Angela,' Mrs Mackenzie replied civilly. 'Why aren't you at school?' she asked.

'Same reason as *her*,' Angela replied, pointing at Lucy Jane. 'Holidays.' And she stuck out her tongue at Lucy Jane so quickly that Mrs Mackenzie didn't notice and only saw her smile sweetly.

'My mother wants me to try to be on the television,' she said to Lucy Jane. 'Auditions are on Monday and I'll be there.'

Lucy Jane was envious. She wondered if there would be any point in going if Angela and every girl in the

16

village was going to be there as well. Then she thought – "why not?"

As Lucy Jane and her grandmother left the shop Angela called after her, 'Orange Pips to you,' and once again she stuck out her tongue behind Mrs Mackenzie's back. Lucy Jane looked back over her shoulder and gave Angela a sheepish smile. She was glad there was a girl of her own age living so near. Lucy Jane immediately liked her. She hoped there would be parts for both of them.

The next morning passed slowly. Lucy Jane could only think about finding an excuse to get out of the house on Monday so that she could go to the audition. So, later, when she and her grandmother were eating lunch she suggested, 'Granny, shall I go down to the village on my own and collect your newspaper for you on Monday?'

'That's very sweet of you, dear,' Mrs Mackenzie said, 'very sweet.'

'Then I really can go?' Lucy Jane asked, anxious to get her grandmother's total approval of the idea. Now at last there was a real adventure to look forward to; all she had to do was make sure that her grandmother didn't change her mind.

When her grandmother answered, 'Yes, dear, of course you can go,' Lucy Jane's stomach turned over in excitement.

Lucy Jane Tadworth was going to an audition and maybe she'd get the part and become a television star. 'Jumping cactus,' she said happily. The excitement was more than she could bear.

3

The Audition

On Monday morning Lucy Jane made her way nervously along the cobbled streets of Rockleigh with the newspaper article clutched in her hand, frantically searching for someone to show her the way to the village school. The school hall was a pinkish grey building at the far end of the village near St John's Kirk. She was already a little late, so she ran as fast as she could. When she arrived, very hot and out of breath, she was amazed to find that the hall was completely empty. Was she the first child there? She stood for a moment feeling a little frightened and wondered if she had come to the right place on the right day.

She looked at the ceiling. Had she remembered all the details on the poster? As she stood alone in the big empty building she felt more and more worried then she rushed outside. Above the hall she read the words, 'St John's Kirk Hall 1872'.

'Oh, no! Oh yes! Oh rats!' Lucy Jane exclaimed as she realized her mistake. 'I'm not at the school at all.' And she hurried from the courtyard into the street. 'I shall miss my chance!'

Suddenly she noticed hoards of children gathering outside a large building further down the street, and ran towards them.

As she neared the group, rather out of breath, she was overwhelmed by the noise. The sound of anxious mothers pushing and jostling their daughters to get them to the front of the queue to be the first to be seen by the director almost deafened her.

Lucy Jane looked very small as she stood at the edge of the crowd wondering if she should have dared to come on her own. She was about to turn back when suddenly the whole crowd of mothers and children surged forward. One of the girls grabbed Lucy Jane by the hand and she was dragged along with them until eventually they all found themselves squashed into the school hall.

Once inside, a man with a loud hailer was calling:

'Mothers, stand back, please. All the girls in straight lines on this side of the hall.'

The girls rushed obediently, anxious to do as they were told. There was a lot of barging and shoving and Lucy Jane found herself squashed into the back line where no one could see her. She looked around. All the girls seemed ill at ease whether they were looking scruffy or overdressed. They coughed, fidgeted, shuffled their feet, and some did not appear to know why they were there. They looked at John Hall, the television director, then at David Savage, the producer from America, who was in charge of the business side of the production, and then at Jack, Mr Hall's personal assistant – P.A. as he was called – who was very tall. As the men walked up and down the lines, the girls followed them with their eyes and waited nervously. Lucy Jane was hoping they would notice her squashed between two big girls at the back.

It was obvious by the expression on John Hall's face that none of the girls was exactly what he wanted for the part of the younger sister. For one thing no one looked like Andy, the boy who was going to play Daniel, the brother. At last the director pointed to two girls in the first row, Angela and a shy girl called Josslyn in a red dress, and whispered to the producer.

'These two little girls in the front are best, and their hair is long.' Then he added to his P.A., 'Jack, I'd like to test the girls on film on Thursday morning.' He paused. 'Please give them each the sheet of paper with the lines they need to study and ask their mothers to help them learn the words and tell them we will collect them on Thursday morning to take them to the make-up caravan.'

Lucy Jane pushed her way forward saying, 'No one's audited me yet.'

'No one's *audited* you, young lady, as we are not "auditing" or counting the money here, we are AUDITIONING which is quite a different thing.' Jack laughed, looking down at Lucy Jane.

Some of the girls giggled and one or two of the bolder mothers pushed forward saying, 'What about my daughter? She'd be lovely on television and she's got long hair and you've not looked at her.'

Lucy Jane wondered if she should have spoken.

'Quiet, please,' Jack called. 'Let the director think.'

But the director said nothing. So Lucy Jane, still looking very hot and messy, decided to stand her

ground and piped up again and said in a quaking voice, 'No one has looked at me yet and I've danced in the ballet.'

Two of the larger girls fell over each other laughing and Angela came over to Lucy Jane and whispered, 'Your grandma won't want to hear you've been behaving like this.'

Lucy Jane felt a feeling of panic. Then suddenly the director looked down at Lucy Jane and said, 'Where have you come from? Get in line with the other girls. I've chosen the girls who we are going to test, but let me look at you. Take off your glasses.'

Lucy Jane nervously did as she was told.

'Test?' she repeated. 'You mean school work?' she added fearfully.

'No, no!' the director replied flatly. 'It means see you on film.' Then he turned to Mr Savage and said, 'I know she's a bit small, but she does look like Andy.' Mr Savage agreed. 'Well, young lady, do you want to test?'

Lucy Jane nodded her head, although she wasn't at all sure what she was saying 'Yes' to. Why, she wondered, was she suddenly asked to test when she hadn't even auditioned?

'I thought this was an audition,' she blurted out.

Mr Hall didn't reply and just said kindly, 'Stand by the side of the girl with long hair in the red dress. Now I want all three girls to move forward.' Lucy Jane and Josslyn moved into place as the director walked further down the hall and stood staring at the girls from afar. Then he repeated, 'You, the girl with freckles, please step forward.' Angela obediently stood beside Lucy Jane and Josslyn, who was nervously fiddling with the hem of her dress.

'So you want to be on the telly as well,' Angela said to

Lucy Jane, looking her up and down.

Lucy Jane nodded eagerly. She quickly crossed her fingers that Mr Hall would choose her.

As she stood with her arms straight down by her side, holding her glasses, she tried to make herself look as tall as Angela and Josslyn. She blinked up at Mr Hall with her large brown eyes. Suddenly she felt frogs jumping in her head, mice in her feet, feathers in her tummy. 'Jumping cactus,' she said to herself. 'What would Mummy think of this?'

'What do you want to be on the telly for?' Angela asked.

The director continued looking at the girls for some time, his head on one side and his hands stroking his chin.

'Same reason as you,' Lucy Jane whispered, wishing Angela would not ask questions at such an important moment. There was a long silence and at last Mr Hall said, 'All right, these three girls can test on Thursday,' and turned away to talk to Mr Savage.

There was a burst of sighs and groans and moans from the mothers and the girls that hadn't been chosen.

Lucy Jane jumped up and down, her heart beating with excitement. Josslyn was still fiddling with her dress and Angela was making faces at one of the other girls. Then Jack, Mr Hall's personal assistant, gave them each a sheet of paper with the words they had to learn by Thursday, and asked for the girls' names, addresses and telephone numbers.

'If your parents are not waiting for you, we'll contact them by telephone this evening and explain everything,' he said.

'Your name and number, please?' Jack asked Lucy Jane.

Lucy Jane didn't want to give her grandmother's telephone number.

'I think the telephone is broken,' Lucy Jane lied and then added quickly, 'Please can I have your number instead and I can telephone you?'

Jack said that he felt sure there would be no need to telephone, but took Lucy Jane's number anyway, saying, 'Just be at the Castle at 12.30 pm on Thursday. You will be the last girl to test.' And he handed her the sheet of paper with the lines she had to learn.

Lucy Jane nodded, her head swimming with excitement. She was so happy she wanted to skip around the room. Already her mind was racing, planning how she could best leave the house on Thursday without her grandmother knowing what she was up to.

When she reached the farmhouse she suddenly remembered she had forgotten her excuse! She hadn't bought the newspaper! But fortunately Granny was on the telephone and had forgotten all about it. As soon as she saw Lucy Jane she asked her to come in and speak to her mother.

Poor Lucy Jane was bursting to tell her mother her news, but of course all she could say was that a television film was being made at Rockleigh.

Although she missed her mother and father she didn't feel homesick and she knew no matter how long she was away they would always be happy to see her and love her just as much when she got home.

That night at supper Lucy Jane decided it was best to tell her grandmother about her plans, so she rather tentatively mentioned the television film.

'Granny,' she said slowly as she finished her spaghetti and tomato sauce. 'What would you think if I had the chance to be in the television film?'

'Well, dearie,' her granny replied seriously, 'I wouldn't think anything of it, as it's not likely to happen, is it?' she said, looking straight at Lucy Jane.

'But supposing it was,' Lucy Jane continued eagerly.

'Well, as far as I'm concerned you are here to get some roses in your cheeks,' Mrs Mackenzie replied slowly, 'so doing a film would not be a good idea.' And it looked to Lucy Jane as if the subject was closed.

Wednesday dragged by. Lucy Jane was still thinking how she could sneak away on Thursday, when at lunch Mrs Mackenzie announced, 'I have to visit a sick friend on Thursday. You can either come with me or stay with Mrs Tamm.'

Lucy Jane held her breath. This was more luck than she could have hoped for.

'I think I'll stay with Tammy, if that's all right with you, Granny,' she replied, keeping her eyes down so that her grandmother should not know how anxious she was to stay in Rockleigh.

'All right, dearie,' Mrs Mackenzie said. 'I shall be back by six, so wait for me for supper, but it's best if you have lunch with Tammy.'

'Rabbits,' Lucy Jane thought. 'That ruins it!' But she still went up to her bedroom to learn her lines.

Lucy Jane was testing for the part of Isabella, the youngest of four children, two girls and two boys, who lived in Rockleigh Castle in 1872. The children's wicked uncle was also their guardian as their parents had died in a hunting accident when the children were small. He planned to get rid of the children by poisoning them so that he could take all the money their parents had left them and keep the castle for himself.

Lucy Jane had only acted twice before: one year she

had been a sheep and the following year she had played Mary in the Nativity Plays at School. She liked acting, and it came as naturally to her as the ballet. So the idea of playing a tragic, sick girl on the television appealed to her very much.

When her grandmother came upstairs to say goodnight, Lucy Jane was standing in front of the mirror acting out her part with all her heart.

'What on earth are you doing, dearie?' her grandmother asked, amazed to see Lucy Jane gesturing in the mirror. Lucy Jane didn't answer and jumped into bed. In the panic, she dropped her lines. Her grandmother immediately spotted them.

'Lucy Jane?' she asked. Lucy Jane's heart stopped; then started beating very fast as she nodded to her grandmother.

'How many times must I tell you, dearie, not to be untidy? Pick up that piece of paper and put it into the wastepaper basket.'

Lucy Jane scampered out of bed and did as she was told.

'Now go to sleep, dearie – I want you to look bonny when Mummy and Daddy come. If I come in again I do not want to find you out of bed,' and then she kissed Lucy Jane goodnight.

'Yes, Granny,' Lucy Jane replied meekly as she hugged and kissed her grandmother, and thought happily, 'I miss my cuddles with Mummy but Granny's a good second best.' Then she snuggled under the covers to dream about the test.

'Now, Lucy Jane, dearie,' Mrs Mackenzie said the next morning at breakfast, 'I want you to be a good girl and do whatever Mrs Tamm tells you; I should be home at about tea-time but it depends.'

'On what?' Lucy Jane asked nervously.

'Well, darling, all sorts of things, but one thing is certain, I shan't be too late.'

'What do you mean by "late"?' Lucy Jane questioned again.

'Well, dearie, whatever happens I should be home before seven.'

'Seven,' Lucy Jane thought. 'Jumping cactus! If only Granny's friend can keep her there until *seven*, I will have time to go to the castle, do my test, and be home before Granny returns.'

Mrs Mackenzie left after breakfast and Lucy Jane skipped about excitedly longing to leave for the castle. She went into the kitchen to see Mrs Tamm. As she stood watching her roll the pastry she stroked the dog pensively wondering how she could tell Mrs Tamm she wanted to go out.

'Tammy,' Lucy Jane said suddenly. 'Please may I go down to the newsagent's later and see Angela? Daddy gave me five pounds and I'd like to buy a book to read.'

Everyone in the village knew Lucy Jane so she would be quite safe and Mrs Tamm agreed.

When Lucy Jane arrived at the newsagent's, Angela had already left for the castle and her mother was serving at the counter.

'What can I do for you, Lucy? Where's your grandmother?'

'She's gone out for the day, so I've come to see Angela,' Lucy Jane replied, half truthfully in a small voice.

'Well, she's gone to do a television test. She won't be back till later. Why don't you go up to the castle?'

Lucy Jane thought for a moment. 'What's the time?' she asked.

'Oh, about eleven,' Mrs Davies replied.

'Do you think,' Lucy Jane continued carefully, 'we could ring Mrs Tamm and tell her I've gone to see Angela at the castle?'

Mrs Davies asked, 'Have you got the money for the call?'

'Yes, I've got five pounds from Daddy,' Lucy Jane replied quickly.

'Well, it won't cost that, but everything costs money these days, so you'd better buy a comic or something and with the change we can make the call.'

Lucy Jane chose a small book about shells.

'I'd like this, please,' she said, holding up the book and trying to reach across the counter with her money. 'And now can we telephone?' she asked.

Mrs Davies took Lucy Jane's money, slipped the book into a paper bag and gave Lucy Jane her change, minus 10p for the telephone.

'Come into the back of the shop and we'll ring.' Lucy Jane followed behind Mrs Davies like a little dog.

'Oh, hallo, dear, it's Renee – I've got Mrs Mackenzie's granddaughter Lucy here. She wants to visit Angela at the castle. Is it all right with you?'

Lucy Jane was afraid Mrs Tamm would say no.

'OK, dear,' she heard Mrs Davies say as she put down the phone.

Lucy Jane followed her back to the shop and waited anxiously to know what Mrs Tamm had said, but Mrs Davies just carried on unpacking magazines. Lucy Jane could bear the suspense no longer and she said, 'Mrs Davies?'

Mrs Davies stopped and stared at Lucy Jane who looked rather forlorn standing in front of some large jars of sweets that towered over her.

'Well, duckie, what are you waiting for?' Mrs Davies asked. 'Off you go, but be back home by tea – Mrs Tamm's orders.'

'Does that mean that I can go?'

'Yes, yes, don't bother me no more. Run along. Mollie says be back by tea, now.' And Mrs Davies returned to her work.

'Wonderful,' thought Lucy Jane happily. 'I can go to the castle.' And she set off up the hill. Suddenly every thing inside her turned to jelly, her feet felt like marshmallows, her stomach full of feathers and her head seemed alive with frogs jumping in all directions. Her cheeks became hot and red and Lucy Jane smiled to herself as she was sure that her grandmother would think they looked lovely and rosy.

When she arrived, she found a row of large caravans parked on the side of the hill. Lucy Jane had no idea where she should go, so she was relieved when a boy of about twelve came up to her and said, 'You lost?'

'Well, a bit,' Lucy Jane replied.

'Thought as much,' the boy said casually.

'You one of the girls who might play my sister?' the boy asked.

'I don't really know.'

'Thought as much,' the boy said again. 'All the girls they've found have been dopey.'

Lucy Jane was furious. So she looked at him and said, 'Watch what you say because I'm ten now, and I've got a brother.' She didn't add that her brother was only one, couldn't talk and could hardly walk.

'Well, anyway,' the boy said, pointing up the hill, 'you have to go to the hairdressing in that caravan, if you're going to test.'

Lucy Jane nodded and walked away from the boy as quickly as she could. The boy looked after her and mumbled, 'Girls!'

Lucy Jane clambered up the steep caravan steps and when she arrived inside she found Angela already there, sitting in front of the mirror, her newly curled hair tied with long cream satin ribbons. She was wearing a long nightgown with a frill round the bottom and a crocheted shawl round her shoulders. She looked like a character out of a Victorian story book.

'Hallo,' Lucy Jane said quietly. 'Am I late?'

'Depends what you mean by late, Orange Pips,' Angela replied cheerfully.

'Ooh! What *are* they doing to you? You look quite different,' Lucy Jane exclaimed admiringly.

'What do you think they're doing?' Angela replied. 'They're getting me ready to test.' Then she asked grandly, 'Know your lines?' hoping Lucy Jane would say 'No', as she hadn't managed to learn her own. Her mother had been too busy to help her, and also she found it difficult to read.

Lucy Jane looked up at her and nodded sweetly. 'Yes, I think I do,' she said and hunched up her shoulders as much as to say, 'I hope so.'

All the while Joan, the make-up supervisor and hairdresser, was standing over them with her arms folded.

'Come on, girls,' she said finally. 'Enough of this rabbiting. We've got a job to do.'

Lucy Jane looked up surprised, rather taken aback by this tall lady looking very fierce.

'What's your name, young lady?' the tall lady asked.

'Lucy Jane,' she replied meekly.

'Angela, as you're ready, let Lucy Jane sit in the chair. Now, Lucy Jane, you're third on my list. Take off your glasses and let's have a look at you,' and she peered at Lucy Jane.

'Mmmm!' she said slowly. 'At least you're not covered in freckles.'

Angela glanced up fiercely as she got up from the chair.

'Jumping cactus!' Lucy Jane thought as she looked in the big mirror, thrilled at the idea of having make-up on her face again.

'From now on, we'll have a little bit of hush in here,' Joan said to the girls. 'I'm here to do a job and a job I'll do. I've got to get you ready quickly so my assistant Tina can show you where to get into your costume and then take you up to the castle.'

So Angela and Lucy Jane were silent while Joan worked, the serious expression never leaving her face as she transformed Lucy Jane from a messy little tomboy into a Victorian young lady. When she had finished, Lucy Jane put on her glasses and peered at herself in the mirror. Suddenly all the magic of performing in the

ballet came flooding back, the feeling of being special added to the excitement of doing something no one in her family knew about.

'This is going to be like fireworks, butterflies and smarties,' she thought as she studied the powder on her face and looked at the ribbon in her now curly hair. 'This is going to be better than Christmas!' she exclaimed ecstatically to Angela as she jumped out of the make-up chair and grabbed Angela's hand. 'We may be television stars and go to America and meet all the people in Hollywood,' she said as she jumped down.

4

Lucy Jane's Chance

Rockleigh Castle stood imperiously on the hill looking down over the make-up caravan and the village of Rockleigh. The castle wasn't like the ones in picture books, it didn't have a moat or a drawbridge or tower with turrets. It looked more like a huge grey stone mansion with an enormous entrance hall, like many of the castles built in Scotland hundreds of years ago.

But a castle it was. It had four wings, a small ballroom and a great dining hall. Inside, the walls were built of the same grey stone, and the ceiling of the dining hall was carved in dark wood. The ballroom had a very high ceiling painted gold and blue and huge tapestries of horses and men in battle hung on the walls. The furniture was very large and heavy, made of dark carved wood, and covered in material that looked extremely thick and very scratchy. There were also shields and swords and antlers fixed high up all along the walls of the corridors and dusty suits of armour stood at every corner.

Although Lucy Jane was with Angela and Tina, the make-up assistant, she found walking through the castle rather scary.

'Jumping cactus,' she exclaimed, 'I've never seen so many tin men!' Then she added to Angela, 'Hope they're not rusty, otherwise their joints will get stuck if they move about at night, just like the Tin Man in *The Wizard of Oz*.'

They walked on a little and Tina said to the girls as they passed a thick black wooden door, 'They say a man was eaten to death by rats down in that dungeon.'

'Ugh!' Angela screamed.

'I don't believe a man would sit there while rats ate him,' Lucy Jane observed thoughtfully. 'I think it's just a story to make small children frightened like ghosts and dragons and . . . ' she tailed off, not able to think of other things that frightened children.

'You don't live up here, do you?' Angela asked as they walked. 'Where do you come from?'

'London,' Lucy Jane replied.

'Phew! I wouldn't like to live in a smelly noisy place like London. All those houses, cars and people!' Angela replied.

'Yes, it is pretty noisy,' Lucy Jane answered. 'But as I'm used to it, I don't mind.'

Angela looked at her. 'We live over the shop. Handy for my mum. And,' she added suddenly, 'my mother's pretty fierce. She wants me to be in this television film, so she won't be pleased if the director gives you the part instead of me because we need the money!' And she gave a sharp look at Lucy Jane.

'Then I hope you get it,' Lucy Jane said untruthfully, 'as it doesn't really make any difference to me.' She paused. 'I'm like that,' she said, trying to be very grown up. 'Sometimes I'm quite easy. What about you?'

'Oh, my mother says I'm like six cats in a bag – always squealing,' Angela answered, laughing. 'Don't know why.' She threw her head back and laughed. An infectious laugh which made Lucy Jane laugh too.

'Come on, girls,' Tina called over her shoulder. The girls giggled and ran to keep up.

'I think,' Lucy Jane whispered quickly, 'you're what my mother would call full of life. Lively. I like you. I think my little brother would too.'

Suddenly Tina said, 'Got to leave you here. Just remembered, have to go back to collect my make-up box. They're testing in the room at the end of the corridor where you can see all the lights. Don't worry. Jack, the assistant, will tell you what to do, and Joan will be with you,' and she was gone.

'That wasn't very friendly,' Lucy Jane said to Angela, a little frightened. 'We could get lost and never do this test at all.' And they hurried along the corridor.

The room where they were filming was ablaze with bright lights and people bustling everywhere, calling and shouting. 'Move the camera to the right. Get those lights out of the way. Bring the bed closer.'

Lucy Jane entered the room and took a deep breath. 'So this was filming!' she thought as all the magic of the television set enveloped her. It was like no other place in the world and she immediately felt happy and at home in it although it wasn't as colourful or as pretty as Covent Garden. She suddenly realized that her father could have designed the set; she knew he often did do the sets for television films.

The room didn't look at all like a normal room as everything seemed to be in the wrong place. In the middle there was a huge old four-poster bed with

Josslyn lying on a heap of pillows with lights all around her. There was a huge camera moving like a Dalek on wheels, and the large lights were fixed on to tall iron stands, much bigger lights than would ever be used in anyone's sitting room, and although it was daylight the curtains were drawn. The atmosphere in the room was very special suddenly. Lucy Jane squeezed Angela's hand saying, 'Good luck, Miss Orange Pips.'

At that moment Jack, the first assistant, walked over to them and said, 'Come in, come and see the director and he will explain what you have to do.'

Lucy Jane was amazed that so many people were needed.

'Angela and Lucy Jane, is it?' The director John Hall asked kindly as he ambled towards them. He seemed more friendly than at the audition.

'Yes,' they both answered quietly.

'But you can call me Lucy,' Lucy Jane piped in, beaming at Mr Hall, as though she wasn't nervous at all.

'Lucy? Fine,' the director said, smiling. 'Now, I'd like to tell you a little of the story. Well, Isabella, the younger sister, is lying in bed as she has been poisoned by her uncle.'

'Why doesn't she die?' Lucy Jane asked, concerned.

'Because her uncle didn't give her enough poison to kill her, just enough to make her very ill,' Mr Hall answered patiently.

'Good,' Lucy Jane mumbled, relieved. Then Mr Hall continued.

'She calls to her sister Clarissa, who is sleeping in the next room, to come to her rescue, as she is sure she is dying. But we don't see Clarissa in this scene, by the way. Now, all we're doing for the test is the short piece where Isabella is ill in bed calling for her sister. But it's

very dramatic, and it's important that the girl playing Isabella can really show all those things Isabella feels, and act as if she is really ill.'

The girls nodded again, realizing it was much more difficult than just learning the words.

'Although it's a very short scene it requires a *real* actress. Have you learnt your lines?'

Both the girls nodded again.

'Good,' Mr Hall said, 'so wait while Josslyn finishes her test and then I'll be with you.'

And he left Angela and Lucy Jane still holding hands, looking very small beside the big camera.

'Hope I remember my lines,' Angela said suddenly.

'Mm,' Lucy Jane nodded, unable to speak.

Josslyn was lying in bed looking very nervous and very pale.

Suddenly she beckoned to Lucy Jane, who was now standing at the side of the camera. 'Psst,' she whispered to Lucy Jane. 'Come here. What's your name?'

'Lucy Jane,' Lucy Jane replied as softly as she could as now everyone was working very quietly and not talking. Lucy Jane went a little closer and whispered, 'What's yours?'

'Josslyn,' the girl replied. 'Why are you here? Do you want to be on television?'

Lucy Jane thought it rather a strange question. 'Well, sort of, but I like the ballet most,' then she added quietly, 'I was in the *Nutcracker* at Covent Garden once.'

'Were you?' Josslyn replied, impressed, pulling Lucy Jane's sleeve nervously to make her sit on the bed.

'I'm so frightened, I wish you could do the test instead of me,' she pleaded.

'Better not,' Lucy Jane answered. Then added comfortingly, 'Don't worry, these auditions are nothing to worry about. If you do as you're told, I'm sure you'll find it easy.'

'I doubt it,' Josslyn replied. 'I'm only here because my mummy wants me to be on television. She wants me to be famous, but I don't.'

'Never mind, you look pretty in your nightie,' Lucy Jane said sweetly, grateful that her mother wouldn't force her to be on television if she didn't want to be, and she slipped away to wait for her turn. Suddenly Lucy Jane was struck with a feeling of panic; supposing her grandmother had come home? Supposing she or Mrs Tamm came striding into the castle? What would she do? What would she say? She tried to banish these thoughts and watch Josslyn.

Josslyn found it so hard to pretend she was ill that after a little while the producer and director reluctantly agreed it was best to let her go home. Lucy Jane was suddenly afraid. Would this happen to her? She wished her mother was with her; or her little brother so she could hold his hand. His hands were small and squashy and they always made her feel safe.

Angela was the next to test and, as the freckles on her face still showed, Joan was doing her best to hide them with make-up. Angela didn't like it, and complained bitterly, 'Take that sticky sponge off my face, I don't want no silly make-up. Let me be. God gave me freckles and I intend to keep them,' and she pushed Joan away.

The director was now concerned that Angela would also become too distressed to act, so he did his best to calm her down by promising that Joan wouldn't come near her again. Once Angela had recovered, although she couldn't remember her lines very well, she acted in a way that moved everyone. Lucy Jane watched her, full of admiration, while the nerves for her own test grew.

41

The producer Mr Savage, walked over to Angela and enthused, 'I look forward to the "rushes", Angela, and seeing the results of your test on the screen.' Angela beamed. He smiled. And Lucy Jane wished she could go home.

'We'll telephone your parents to let them know the results,' he said to Angela. 'You were very good, but try to concentrate a little more on learning your lines properly in future.'

Angela opened her eyes wide and made a face.

Then John Hall looked at Lucy Jane.

'Lucy Jane,' he called. 'Come here. Now it's your turn, Lucy,' he said, signalling to Jack to join him.

Suddenly Lucy Jane was really nervous. She felt quite hot. Her hair stuck to her forehead and perspiration shone on her face. She climbed into the huge four-poster bed and flopped her head back on to the heap of pillows. Without being asked to start, Lucy Jane tossed her head on the pillow, murmuring the words she had learnt in a soft, moaning voice, as though she was really dying.

'I think I've been poisoned, Clarissa.'

Mr Hall suddenly noticed that Lucy Jane was already playing the scene and stopped speaking in mid-sentence.

'Well, this little one is keen,' he remarked as he walked towards the camera.

'Water, Clarissa, bring me water. I'm dying of thirst,' Lucy Jane sighed.

Then she heard the director's voice call, 'Good. Good, now start again, Lucy,' and added to the camera, 'Roll 'em,' and the camera started filming Lucy Jane.

'Now, imagine your sister Clarissa has come into the room,' the director's voice whispered. 'Sit up, and call

42

out to her again.'

Lucy Jane obeyed his directions as though she had been acting all her life.

'Good. Cut,' Mr Hall said, and the camera stopped rolling.

'I'm an actress!' Lucy Jane thought excitedly and lay in the bed relieved that for the moment it was over, and waited to be told what to do next. But no one came near her.

The lights were turned off and everyone scurried about carrying on with their jobs as though she wasn't there.

'She was better than I thought she'd be,' the director said enthusiastically to Mr Savage. 'I only really tested her as she had the cheek to say she'd been ignored at the audition and, of course, because of her long hair. Excellent hair when it's not in plaits.'

Marty Savage nodded and puffed his cigar.

'Better ask her to do the scene again, though,' and he signalled to Jack.

'Once more, boys!' Jack cried and suddenly all the bright lights went on with a loud cracking sound. Then everyone rushed around and started straightening the pillows, pulling the bed cover and fussing with Lucy Jane's hair.

'Now, Lucy,' the director said. 'Just once more before you go home.'

'Silence, everyone!' Jack yelled and everyone was quiet.

Again Lucy Jane felt quite nervous. When the director called, 'OK, Lucy, action!' she started to act the scene again. As she said her lines she found her mind wandering. Would she be chosen for the part and, if she was, would her father be pleased that she, too, worked in television? She wondered what her granny would think. Granny!

Suddenly in the middle of the scene she jumped out of the bed in a panic, saying, 'What's the time? Granny will be back in a moment. I must go!' and she dashed towards the door.

'Come back!' the director called fiercely. 'Get back into bed, Lucy, we haven't finished.'

Lucy Jane obediently jumped back into bed, still worried about her grandmother. But fortunately she

acted the scene even better the second time and Mr Hall was very pleased.

'Good, cut,' he called. 'Thank you, Lucy, we're finished.'

'OK, chaps. It's a wrap!' the first assistant's voice yelled through the room.

Suddenly everyone was galvanised into noisy activity as the technicians packed up to go.

'What about me?' Lucy Jane's small voice pierced through the noise. 'Is anyone going to wrap me up?' The entire crew burst out laughing. By now Lucy Jane was dreadfully worried that if she didn't hurry she wouldn't get home before her granny.

Suddenly the producer and director remembered her.

'Sorry, Lucy, we were so busy talking. You were very good – and when we see the "rushes" we'll know who looks the most like Andy and then we can choose who will be the best Isabella.'

'Do you think it might be me?' Lucy Jane asked anxiously.

The director didn't reply, and just shrugged and smiled.

'I must rush now,' Lucy Jane said politely, and dashed out of the room. She flew down the corridor as quickly as she could, hair ribbons flying, nightie held high. When she arrived at the caravan she was panting and out of breath.

'So far,' Lucy Jane thought excitedly as she took off her nightie, 'I've managed an audition *and* a test for television without anyone knowing.'

She dressed hurriedly, then suddenly her heart missed a beat. What would she say to her grandmother when she got home? What if Mr Hall's assistant phoned her? She ran back up the hill to look for him.

'Excuse me, Jack,' she panted. 'If you ring my house, please could you ask to speak to me?' She paused. 'Me, Lucy Jane, and no one else.'

'OK,' Jack said and smiled.

'I mean, please don't leave a message with *anyone else*, just speak to *me*,' Lucy Jane insisted.

'OK,' he said again.

Reassured, Lucy Jane waved him goodbye and raced down the hill again as fast as she could.

'Where are you going, young lady?' he called.

'Home.'

'No, no,' Jack said. 'You wait here a moment and the producer's car will take you home.'

'It's all right,' Lucy answered quickly. 'I'll go on my feet.' The last thing in the world she wanted was to be seen arriving home in the producer's car. All the cars had 'Star Television Films' written on a large white card on the windscreen, and that would certainly have given the game away.

'Wait,' Jack called.

'No, I'd rather not,' Lucy Jane shouted back and ran on down the hill towards home as fast as she could.

Fortunately, Lucy Jane arrived at the farmhouse well before her grandmother, so she walked into the kitchen as though nothing had happened. Mrs Tamm was so busy putting jam in the sponge cake she didn't even look up.

'Hello, Tammy,' Lucy Jane said and casually wandered around the kitchen.

'Had a nice time at the castle?' Mrs Tamm asked. This made Lucy Jane rush to the mirror at the back door to see if any make-up was left on her face. Luckily she still looked as untidy as when she'd left the house.

'Brilliant, thanks, Tammy,' she answered at last.

All of a sudden Lucy Jane let out a little start as though she had seen a mouse.

Mrs Tamm dropped the knife she was washing up and looked up. 'What on earth is it, Lucy?' Mrs Tamm asked anxiously.

'Nothing, Tammy,' Lucy Jane said, not telling the truth. 'Nothing, just a frog jumped into my mind and gave me a start,' she said, and went out of the back door into the garden as quickly as she could.

'Help!' she said to herself. 'Granny's so against this television film. Maybe I won't get the part anyway, because I stopped acting in the middle of the scene.' She stood still a moment looking very worried. 'Perhaps they'll think I'm always stopping acting when I shouldn't.' She felt quite sick at the thought that she might have ruined her chances. Now all she could do was wait. She knew it was going to seem a long wait. But in the meantime she had to be sensible and try and win over her granny. She went back into the kitchen.

'Can you keep a secret, Tammy?' Lucy Jane asked anxiously over tea.

'Depends,' Mrs Tamm said, not really listening to the little girl's conversation. 'Depends,' she repeated slowly, still finishing the cake.

Lucy Jane thought for a moment. Suddenly she took a deep breath and announced, 'Tammy, this afternoon, while I was out, the camera rolled on me and . . . '

Mrs Tamm looked up aghast. 'You were run over by a camera! Lord have mercy!' she exclaimed and she fell back into her chair making it squeak.

'No, no,' Lucy assured her. 'Camera rolling means the camera is working and is photographing what you do.'

'Why in heaven's name would it be doing that?' Mrs Tamm asked. 'What were you doing that had to be photographed?' Mrs Tamm looked very worried.

'I was doing a TEST,' Lucy Jane said happily.

'A test – a school test?' the housekeeper asked, surprised.

'No. No, a test for television,' Lucy Jane replied.

'A television TEST!' Mrs Tamm exclaimed loudly. 'Lord have mercy.'

At that moment the door opened and Granny stood in the doorway.

'What are you "Lord have mercying" about, Mollie?' Mrs Mackenzie asked as she walked over to kiss her granddaughter. 'Hello, sweetheart,' she said. 'Have you had a good afternoon?'

There was a silence. Nobody spoke. Lucy Jane went very red in the face, and Mrs Tamm said quietly, 'I don't really know, Mrs Mackenzie. It's a secret, but I think your granddaughter got run over by a camera!'

Mrs Mackenzie rushed to see if Lucy Jane was all right.

'Lucy, darling, are you all right?' she said, inspecting the child from top to bottom. 'What happened. Don't tell me you're hurt, dearie.'

Lucy Jane wanted to laugh as she stood between the two women fussing over her.

'No, Granny, I'm not hurt,' she said and took another deep breath. This time she tried to explain to her grandmother what had really happened to her. When Mrs Mackenzie had heard the whole story, she had to sit down, she was so surprised. Lucy Jane was so worried she rushed to get her granny a glass of water.

'You mean to say you went to the audition in the

village hall, and did a test without Mollie or myself knowing?' Lucy Jane's grandmother asked flabbergasted.

'Yes, Granny,' she said. 'I haven't made you ill, have I?' she asked, worried. 'I loved the ballet so much and I thought it would be an adventure like that.'

Lucy Jane was silent for a moment. 'An adventure like you had when you were little and went to work in a circus in the holiday.' Then she asked, concerned, 'What are you going to do if I do get the part? Will you let me do it?'

Mrs Mackenzie took Lucy Jane by the hand and said gently, 'I was eighteen when I helped in the circus and all I did was clean out the ponies and my mother was very angry.'

'But those days were different,' Lucy Jane said sagely. 'At least you had an adventure, Granny,' she added, hoping Mrs Mackenzie would see her point of view.

There was a long pause. Mrs Tamm carried on clearing up the tea things. Lucy Jane didn't move. And Mrs Mackenzie sat shaking her head, saying, 'What a little adventurer. My word, what spirit,' and, 'Oh dear, how naughty,' over and over again.

At last Mrs Mackenzie sighed. 'Well, it's no good worrying about spilt milk, dearie. Let's not talk about it any more today — I'll think about the whole thing tonight. But, Lucy darling,' she added, 'I am not keen – you are here to have a holiday and that's what I want you to have.'

'Think about it!' Lucy Jane said to herself. Lucy Jane already had thought about it and she knew that whatever her grandmother said, she was determined not to give up her chance of being on television, with or without anyone knowing.

5

An Unexpected Turn

The following day Lucy Jane waited for the television company to call. After breakfast she did her ballet practice and barre exercises in front of the mirror in her bedroom, then she put on her trainers ready to play her secret game – to see how many times she could hop around the house on one leg without falling over.

Each hundred hops gave her a wish for someone she really liked most in the world. First, her mother.

'Hop, Chop, Mop, Stop, Lop, Pop, Mummy is the top.' She puffed as she hopped her way round the house, all the time making sure that if the telephone went she would hear it.

'Skip, Trip, Flip, Dip, Lip, Zip, Rip, Daddy is the best pip,' she puffed again.

On and on and on she hopped until finally after she had done over three thousand hops her legs were so tired she flopped down on to the grass too exhausted to worry if the telephone rang or not.

Suddenly, the phone did ring. She rushed into the house saying, 'Skip it to me, Granny – I mean, give it to me – I know it's for me.'

'It *must* be,' she thought, hoping with all her might that it was Star Television Films.

But Mrs Mackenzie picked up the receiver so Lucy Jane had to wait patiently while her grandmother took the call.

'Yes, yes. I see,' Mrs Mackenzie said. 'I'll tell her.' There was a pause then, 'No, I'm sure she won't mind at all. Thank you for calling,' and she put down the receiver. Lucy Jane looked at her grandmother; she felt her heart beating so fast it was hard for her to think.

Nothing was said for a moment, then at last Lucy Jane questioned anxiously, 'Has Angela got the part and not me?' She couldn't bear to hear her grandmother's answer. She felt half tearful and half relieved.

'Yes, Lucy darling, I'm afraid she has. But I expect you're second choice.'

For some reason Lucy Jane found it hard to speak. The news made her heart sink and she felt strangely sad and quite dizzy. This was the first time that she had had to come to terms with a disappointment of this kind. She wanted so much to be brave. Had she been alone, she would have cried and cuddled the koala and her 'tickly rug', but there was Granny and she knew how she had been very brave in the war and she wanted to be like her.

'It's funny,' she said at last to her grandmother, a lump in her throat, 'I didn't know I wanted to be on the silly old television so much. Now I know I'm not, I wish I was. But as I am ten,' she added seriously, 'it's better that I'm upset rather than Angela's mother, because they need the money and although Daddy's always saying we haven't got enough, maybe they need it more than we do.'

Lucy Jane walked over and picked up the cat who was sitting on the armchair by the unlit fire and whispered, 'Come on, cat, let's go into the garden and look for mice.' She was about to leave the room when her grandmother went over and put her arm round her and said, 'Most things happen for the best, dearie. Most things teach you something, even if it's only how to be second.' She gave Lucy Jane a squeeze.

'Yes,' Lucy Jane said, bravely stopping the tears. 'I'm always learning how to be second at school, sometimes even *tenth*, but I expect I'll get used to it,' she added, giving her granny a brave smile. 'You see,' she continued earnestly, 'it makes me more determined and Mummy says that's good.' She paused a moment. 'Granny, please give me a kiss.' And with that she put her arms round her granny's neck and gave her a hug to show she was grown up and reluctantly put the idea of being in the television film out of her head, unless of course there was a miracle.

All the following week as Lucy Jane was feeling a little homesick Granny was very kind and took Lucy Jane on picnics, played Dominoes with her and they went to see a film. But unfortunately going to the cinema or watching television reminded Lucy Jane of being 'second'.

By the end of the week Mrs Tamm had nearly taught Lucy Jane to make pastry on her own and she had even made an apple pie. She was just about to ring her mummy to tell her about it, when Angela's freckled face suddenly appeared at the kitchen window.

'Want to come and see me act tomorrow, Orange Pips?' she said as she sauntered in through the back door, almost tripping over Mrs Tamm's dog.

53

Lucy Jane wasn't at all sure she wanted to go.

'Not really,' replied Lucy Jane. 'I'm very busy with Mrs Tamm.'

'Yes, but you won't be busy tomorrow,' Angela said. 'Pastry doesn't take for ever.'

Lucy Jane looked at her friend. She liked Angela and in her heart she was annoyed with herself for not wanting to go and watch her act.

'Well, if you do change your mind and want to come to have lunch on *location* and watch me,' Angela said grandly, 'my car will pick you up at 8.30 tomorrow morning and take you to the castle. The producer said I could bring a friend.'

Mrs Tamm, who was listening, bent down and whispered encouragingly, 'Go on, go and see your friend tomorrow – it'll be a day out,' she said.

'All right,' Lucy Jane said, shrugging her shoulders. 'If you really think I should go, Tammy, I'll go,' and she carried on helping washing up the pastry bowl.

'That's settled then,' said Angela gleefully. 'OK, Orange Pips. Don't forget, about 8.30,' and she skipped from the room and out of the back door. As Lucy Jane watched Angela race down the drive towards Rockleigh, her beautiful golden-brown hair flowing and shining in the sun, she felt pleased that Angela was really her friend.

For some reason Lucy Jane found it hard to sleep that night. She still had a strange feeling that something special was about to happen.

As they drove up the hill to the castle where all the caravans were parked, there was a great deal of excitement going on outside the make-up caravan. Joan, the make-up supervisor, was standing on the caravan step throwing her arms to the skies and sighing, 'I don't believe it. Heaven help me. I don't believe this!'

'Come on, Lucy,' the driver said as he put on the brake. 'Let's see what this drama is.' And they got out of the car and walked to the caravan. As they did so Joan pushed past Lucy Jane and the driver and clutched Mr Hall's arm as he came running up the hill.

'You won't believe this, John,' she said, pulling the director towards the caravan. 'You just won't believe this.' And she flung open the caravan door and announced, 'Look!'

For a moment Mr Hall didn't want to look, fearing what he might see. Then he let out a gasp and exclaimed, 'My word, what on earth has happened?'

Angela was sitting in the make-up chair, grinning at him in the mirror from ear to ear. Her beautiful long golden-brown hair was gone. Her head looked like a coconut and, on her left cheek, she had a large, red-looking cut.

'I got fed up with all this hairdressing business each morning,' Angela explained, 'so I chopped it off to make it easier. Problem is,' she added, 'I cut my face as well.'

'The problem is,' John Hall said, controlling his anger, 'we can't work with you today as you look completely different.'

'Why does that matter?' Angela said, smiling.

'Because, my dear,' he answered carefully, 'CONTINUITY. Continuity is so that everything in the story appears in the right order.' And he looked very cross indeed.

'So what?' Angela butted in. 'What does short hair matter?'

'We can't have you with long hair and no scar one

minute and looking like a scarecrow with a cropped head the next,' the director said, red in the face. He glanced at Joan sitting at the other end of the caravan, clutching her head in her hands and moaning, 'I don't believe this – I don't believe it.'

Lucy Jane in the meantime had managed to edge her

way into the caravan to have a closer look at Angela. She stood huddled in the corner, amazed.

'Joan,' the director said quietly, 'we had better have a talk.' And he signalled to Joan to join him outside the caravan.

While they talked outside, Lucy Jane stayed inside and asked, 'Why did you do it, Ange? You look so different – you won't look the same girl in the story without your lovely hair.'

'I don't see why not,' Angela said indignantly. 'People cut their hair in real life all the time.'

'Yes,' Lucy Jane answered, her head on one side, 'but in a television story you can't cut your hair unless the story says so, and anyway, I think you're supposed to look Victorian.'

'Oh, tosh!' Angela replied sharply. 'Who wants to look old-fashioned anyway? All those silly hair ribbons and curls.'

Lucy Jane didn't answer and the girls were silent for a moment. They could just hear the voices outside.

'There's nothing else for it,' they heard Mr Hall say, 'except try and work without her today and then tonight decide if we recast. If we do, how much does it mean we'll have to reshoot?' And he looked very worried while he and Joan worked out what scenes they would have to redo.

At that moment the caravan door opened and a very serious-looking director stood in the doorway.

'Well, we have a big problem,' John Hall said slowly, 'and there seems only one way to solve it as far as today is concerned.' He stopped for a moment and took a deep breath.

'Come out here, girls,' he said, and told them to sit on the caravan step beside him.

When they had both sat down he took hold of each of their hands and again started to explain. 'The problem is this, Angela. You don't look like the same girl and we don't have time to get a wig made as it would take over three weeks and even if we did have time, that cut on your face will show and you didn't have a mark on your cheek when we started.' He stopped and sighed. 'There is only one solution for today. We'll have to put Lucy Jane in your clothes and as her hair looks almost the same as yours was before you cut it . . . ' he paused. Lucy Jane held her breath and Angela cocked her head to one side as the director carried on. 'Well, as Lucy's hair is the same as yours was . . . ' he paused again. Lucy Jane's heart beat faster, and she dared not even look at Mr Hall. 'We'll use the back of Lucy Jane's head today and tonight we'll have a meeting and decide what is the best thing to do.'

Lucy Jane was trembling at the thought that she might be in the television film after all.

'What do you mean?' Angela asked.

'Well,' John Hall continued kindly, 'we may have to recast you, which means find someone else to play your part and then reshoot those scenes we've already shot with you.' He stopped. No one spoke for a moment. Lucy Jane kept her eyes down and tried to battle with a sharp pricking feeling at the back of her eyes. She didn't want to cry, but somehow she felt she might. Angela spoke first.

'Does this mean I won't be in the story any more?' she asked, half tearfully.

'Well, I'm afraid it does,' Mr Hall said gently.

'Will I still get paid?' Angela interjected.

'Yes, you'll still be paid.'

'That's all right then,' she said with a sigh. 'Both

Mum and Dad will be happy.' But she added quietly, 'If I don't play the part, I have a friend who can. My friend Lucy Jane could do it.'

Lucy Jane felt as if she would burst with pleasure.

'Let me be the judge of that,' Mr Hall answered firmly. 'Today we shall use Lucy Jane, but we'll make a decision later.'

Lucy Jane could hardly believe what she had heard.

Mr Hall rose to his feet and squeezed Angela's hand and then Lucy Jane's. 'Now, get ready, Lucy Jane,' he said kindly, not showing how worried he really was. 'Angela, you can stay and watch us working if you want to.'

'Will someone tell my parents?' Angela asked, concerned.

'And mine?' Lucy Jane added.

'Yes, don't worry. My assistant will ring and the producer will probably go and explain everything to your family,' Mr Hall said comfortingly.

'Phew,' Angela let out a huge sigh. In fact, inside, Angela felt rather relieved. She'd had all the fun and excitement of getting the part, and she was to be paid for it, so her mother would be happy, but there'd be none of the bother of learning lines. 'This suits me nicely,' she said. 'Learning lines and reading is so hard and boring. I hate it. I'm very bad at it at school. But,' she added cheerfully, 'I expect you are clever and like reading, old Orange Pips.'

'Oh, Ange!' Lucy Jane answered. 'Aren't you upset?'

'No, Orange Pips, not a bit,' she said brightly. 'Well, Mr Hall,' Angela said, her head cocked up at him, 'I expect it's all for the best,' and she laughed.

John Hall looked at her and said, 'Angela, this is not for the best and if you'll excuse a rude expression, it's a damned nuisance,' and he looked sternly at the two girls.

Lucy Jane didn't move. Then Mr Hall touched her shoulder saying, 'Come on, Lucy, it looks as if you'll be on television after all, even if it's only the back of your head. Run along with Angela to the wardrobe and let's get you into her clothes.'

Lucy Jane looked up at Mr Hall and smiled a nervous smile, then tripped off behind Angela to the wardrobe caravan to chance.

'Fancy this happening to you,' Angela said as she helped Lucy Jane into the long white cotton petticoat with a large frill on the bottom. 'You won't like the dress, it's got wee bones in it to make it stiff all around the chest, and it's ever so tight at the waist.'

'I'm lucky your dress fits me at all,' Lucy Jane replied, feeling quite dizzy with happiness.

The black leather button boots were a little tight on Lucy Jane but Angela assured her that that was how they were supposed to feel.

Then Marion, the costume assistant, came into the caravan and exclaimed when she saw Lucy Jane, 'What on earth are you doing in Angela's clothes?' Then she noticed Angela's hair and let out a cry.

'Thomasina, Thomasina,' she called to the supervisor who was outside. 'Come here quickly.'

Thomasina, who was plump and jolly, with straight, thick black hair cut in a bob, came bustling into the caravan.

'What in the world is going on?' she said.

Lucy Jane piped up first to defend them. 'Don't be cross. Mr Hall asked me to wear Angela's clothes, because Angela has cut her hair.'

'No one tells me anything,' Thomasina grumbled, and Marion raised her eyes to the ceiling in horror. Thomasina immediately checked that all Lucy Jane's clothes were properly hooked up and that the large, dark blue sash was tied firmly around her waist with a floppy bow hanging at the back. Then she placed a blue and white cotton gingham pinafore over Lucy Jane's head.

Thomasina mumbled, 'All this chopping and

changing, when we've only just started. That's children for you! Still, it's not your fault, love,' she added kindly as she fluffed out Lucy Jane's dress. She gave Angela and Lucy a quick look as much as to say she thought it was a pretty poor show.

Lucy Jane in turn gave Angela a look and Angela could see by the twinkle in Lucy Jane's eyes that she thought Thomasina's grumbling was rather fun, but not a bit like her aunt, who was always laughing.

'My aunt is a wardrobe mistress at Covent Garden,' Lucy Jane announced. 'For the ballet, and she *loves* children,' she finished mischievously.

Thomasina looked at her for a moment, ignored her comment and said as she handed her a long blue hair ribbon, 'Now take this to Joan, and ask her to put it in your hair. Run along, otherwise you'll be late on the set and that's no way to start work on your first day.' And she did smile at the girls then.

When they were outside the caravan, Lucy Jane said, 'I don't want to upset you, Ange, when we've only just become friends.'

'Tosh!' Angela exclaimed. 'You are soft, Lucy! I don't care a bit if it's *you*, but I wouldn't be too pleased if it was some toffee-nosed girl from London, or one of those other dopes at the audition.'

Then Angela clasped Lucy Jane's hand and dragged her from the wardrobe caravan and back to the make-up supervisor. Lucy Jane tried to keep up, nearly falling over her long skirt, as the two girls skipped over the rough grass.

'Follow me and Joan will do your hair,' she said. 'I hope she won't be in a bad mood. At least I'll get some peace this morning.' She giggled as she pushed Lucy Jane into Joan's den.

This time Lucy Jane felt quite frightened as she sat in Joan's large black leather make-up chair with a funny leather cushion to lean her head on. Lucy Jane hadn't noticed last time that the chair looked like a dentist's chair and went up and down. The make-up mirror in front of her had lights all around it and someone had written, 'Good luck, Lucy,' in lipstick in the corner. She looked in the mirror and noticed her face looked very white.

'Now then, what's your name again?' Joan asked kindly.

'Lucy Jane!'

'Ah yes, Lucy Jane – you tested after the other girls last week and someone's put your name on the mirror,' she continued. 'Well, here you are. Not nervous, are you?'

Lucy Jane shook her head. 'No, not yet,' she answered, pretending to be strong. 'I've been in the ballet at Covent Garden,' she added grandly. 'You know, the *Nutcracker* at Christmas – I met the Queen and all the Royal Family.'

Joan assumed she was making it up so she didn't bother to answer. 'Lovely,' she mumbled as she brushed Lucy Jane's hair without looking at her. 'Now, let's curl your hair and see what we can do with you.'

Lucy Jane opened her eyes wide and asked, 'What do you mean, "do with me"?'

'Well, let's see if we can make you look nice,' Joan replied.

'I do look nice,' Lucy retorted. 'My mummy thinks I look very nice sometimes, even if I do wear glasses.'

'It doesn't matter what other people think. Let's see what we can do with your hair,' the make-up supervisor answered flatly and undid Lucy Jane's other plait and brushed it out rather fiercely, knocking her glasses off her nose.

'Put a curl in the ends with these Carmen curlers and you'll look perfect.'

Joan took some heated rollers and rolled Lucy Jane's hair around the hot curlers and clipped it to her head.

'That's finished then, that's all that matters,' Joan said.

'Not to me,' Lucy Jane interrupted. 'All that matters to me is . . . ' she paused. 'What do I really care about, except my parents, my brother, Tilly my cat and the ballet?' She thought for a long time and then decided she didn't want to tell the make-up lady what really mattered to her after all.

'Can I get down from this chair for a moment?' Lucy Jane said. 'I feel stiff.'

'Get down and I'll make you a nice cup of tea while your hair sets,' Joan said smiling.

'That would be nice,' Lucy Jane answered as she wandered around the caravan. She stood on tiptoe to look at all the wigs and peep into the make-up boxes Joan stored in there.

Suddenly there was a bang at the door and one of the assistants called, 'Joan, dear, how long until the new girl's ready? We need her on the set in five minutes.'

'Don't panic,' Joan called back calmly without opening the door. 'She'll be there,' and she carried on making a cup of tea. 'As soon as I've got you ready,' she said to Lucy Jane, 'I've got to get Miss Woods, who plays the faithful servant, ready – so my assistant, Tina, will go up to the set and keep an eye on you.'

Lucy was happy. She would really be in *The Russell Adventure* on television, even if it was only the back of her head that showed!

6

A Second Chance for Lucy Jane

When she arrived, Andy was already standing waiting by the camera. He looked as if he could be Lucy Jane's real elder brother. He had the same kind of bright, sparkly eyes and the same tone of golden-brown hair.

'Hallo,' he said rather gruffly. 'Are you here as "old freckles" Angela has gone and chopped off all her hair?'

'Yes,' Lucy Jane replied, happy that someone was talking to her. 'I'm just standing in for her. No one will see me, just the back of my head.'

'That's funny,' the boy said, looking down at her.

'Well, it's because they're going to try to get a new girl from London or maybe get a wig made for Angela. I can't remember which,' Lucy Jane explained.

'Never mind. Let's hope they don't get either and they choose you,' the boy said pointedly. 'By the way, I'm Andy. Who are you?'

'Lucy Jane.'

'Lucy Jane, eh?' Andy repeated cheerily. 'Nice name,

but then of course you can't judge a girl by her name. I don't like girls that much,' he added quickly.

'You can't judge anybody by their name,' Lucy Jane replied, 'and I think it's silly to say you don't like girls. What about your mother? And what do you know about girls at your age anyway?' Lucy Jane retorted.

After this outburst the two waited silently next to the camera, unable to think of anything more to say.

Suddenly the assistant shouted, 'Artists, please.'

'That's us,' Andy said as he touched Lucy Jane's arm and walked across the set.

They were filming in a large nursery at the castle, a much bigger room than any in Lucy Jane's house. There was a rocking horse and a huge old doll's house made of wood and also a wooden model of the Scottish castle in the story. On the shelves were rag dolls, toys made of tin and wooden painted animals. There were bright lights everywhere with large black cables that looked like huge snakes stretched across the floor, which made it difficult to walk.

'Andy, Lucy,' John Hall called. 'I want you both to be looking out of the nursery window, and when you hear a bang on the door I only want Andy to turn round.'

Andy strolled over to the window to show Lucy Jane that he had understood exactly what Mr Hall meant. Lucy Jane followed. She thought Mr Hall was about the same age as her father. He was slimmer but not so tall, and Lucy Jane thought he looked more handsome, but not so kind as her father. He wore a pair of glasses balanced on his head, which made Lucy Jane smile as she thought they looked like bear's ears.

'Now remember, Lucy, when you hear the knock at the door, don't look round, we mustn't see your face.

Just make a start as though you know it will be your wicked uncle and let Andy turn towards the camera,' John Hall said, and he stood looking at them intently, his hands plunged in the pockets of his dark-blue cord trousers.

'Yes,' Lucy Jane replied, anxious to please the director.

After the two children rehearsed the scene several times, Jack the assistant shouted, 'Quiet, please. SILENCE EVERYONE. This is a take.'

Lucy Jane was completely bewildered. 'Take what?' she asked.

'Silence,' Jack shouted at her.

'Yes,' Lucy Jane said a little louder. 'But, please, take what?'

The director took his hands out of his pockets and walked briskly over to Lucy Jane and said quietly, 'A take means we are going to film and "action" means you are to start acting.' Then he walked behind the camera again. Lucy Jane felt a tear roll down her cheek. She quickly wiped it away.

The children were in the middle of acting the scene when without any warning Angela suddenly skipped straight in front of the camera and over to Lucy Jane saying, 'Terrific, Lucy, you look just like me.'

'Oh, Angela, you've ruined the shot!' the director exclaimed. 'Cut! Cut!' Mr Hall's agitated voice called out. 'Please, Angela, we are filming – come and stand by me. You can chat to Lucy Jane afterwards.'

The rest of the day the filming passed without a hitch, and by the time Jack shouted, 'It's a wrap,' Lucy Jane was feeling quite exhilarated, especially as the director said, 'Well done, thank you, Lucy.' But then he added, 'Nothing has been decided yet though, dear, so don't

expect to get the part.'

Lucy Jane felt disappointed and wished he hadn't said anything.

'What's "it's a wrap" mean?' she asked Andy.

'It means it's time to go home.' He smiled a broad, friendly smile. 'You've been great,' he said. 'Sorry I said I don't like girls – silly really.'

Lucy Jane was grateful that he'd been so nice.

'Will you be here again tomorrow?' Thomasina asked her when she reached the wardrobe caravan.

'I don't know. It depends on whether they can find anyone better,' Lucy Jane replied. Then she called goodbye and jumped down the caravan steps and followed Jack to the car, the magic of the day's events still buzzing in her head.

'Wait till I tell Mummy,' Lucy Jane thought, wanting to see her mummy now more than anything else in the world. 'It's funny,' Lucy Jane thought, 'when I'm with Mummy I don't really remember that she's there, but when I'm not at home I remember her all the time. It must be awful for Angela with a mother who's always worried about money and a father who's so often cross. Where is Angela?'

Angela, as if by magic, immediately appeared from behind the car.

'Hallo, Orange Pips, been waiting for you,' she said smiling.

'Can we go in the same car?' Lucy Jane asked Jack.

'Yes,' he said, 'but you must both sit in the back and behave yourselves as the driver doesn't want any nonsense.'

'Oh no. No nonsense from us!' Lucy Jane said brightly and the two girls scampered into the back of the car.

'Are you all right, Ange?' Lucy Jane asked. 'Not too upset about your hair and me wearing your dress and everything?'

'Oh, Orange Pips, you are silly. I was pleased you had a chance of being on television.'

'Really?' Lucy Jane said gratefully. 'You've been a lot nicer about it than I would have been. Look, Ange! You're home,' Lucy Jane exclaimed as the car stopped outside the newsagent's.

Angela jumped out and called, 'See you soon, Orange Pips.'

'Hope so,' Lucy Jane replied cheerfully and the car drove off before Lucy Jane could say goodbye.

On the rest of the ride home Lucy Jane thought about the day.

'Granny, Granny, guess what?' she called excitedly when she arrived at the farmhouse and rushed into the hall. 'I've been shooting all day,' she announced gleefully.

'What?' her grandmother asked, shocked. 'Shooting, did you say?'

'I was in the television film. Only the back of my head, but you see Angela cut her hair off and I . . . ' she tailed off as she could see her grandmother hadn't understood anything she was trying to say.

'Calmly now, what happened?' Mrs Mackenzie asked slowly. 'Start from the beginning, dearie.'

Lucy Jane took a deep breath and began again. 'Only the back of my head, Granny, as Angela's and my hair are the same colour, but I wore her dress and everything, and Mr Hall said I was good,' and she jumped up and down excitedly.

'Good gracious me,' Mrs Mackenzie sighed, hardly believing her ears. 'Why doesn't anyone tell me?' she asked. 'No one tells me these things and every day something is happening to you.'

'I know. Isn't it lovely?'

'I don't know about lovely. What is your mother going to say? All this rushing about.' And she sat on the sofa and pushed her curly grey hair back from her face.

'Anyway,' Lucy Jane said, 'I haven't got the part yet. But if they can't find anybody in London or get a wig for Angela, I think I may get it. But the director said don't expect to be in it, so we'll have to wait and see.'

All of a sudden Lucy Jane's granny stood up. Lucy Jane was alarmed.

'I think we should ring your mother,' Mrs Mackenzie announced smiling.

'Oh yes, let's call Mummy, let's call Mummy! Everything has been really special, so let's tell Mummy.'

Lucy Jane was so excited when she spoke, she could hardly get the words out. Her mother and father and even Jeremy were all crowded round the other end of the telephone.

'Now,' Lucy Jane said, 'all I have to do is wait to see what happens, but whatever it is,' Lucy Jane added happily, 'if it's as good as the first part of the holiday, it has to be peanut butter and jelly.' And after much blowing of kisses Lucy Jane reluctantly put down the receiver and went upstairs to bed feeling very happy, her head full of dreams and her heart full of hope.

7

A Dream Come True

In the days that followed Lucy Jane could only think about being in *The Russell Adventure*. When the third day passed and there was still no news from Star Television Films, Lucy Jane began to feel there was no hope.

Angela hadn't come to visit her so Lucy Jane decided she'd better go and see Angela.

'Granny,' she said. 'Can I go and get your newspaper for you, and see Angela?'

Unfortunately Mrs Mackenzie had other plans and said, 'No, Lucy, dearie, go upstairs and change, as I want you to come with me to Glasgow to visit my friend Dorothy. She would so like to see you.'

'Rabbits,' thought Lucy Jane. Then she began to wonder if her grandmother had had news from Star Television Films and not told her, or if she had rung the producer and told him she didn't want Lucy Jane to be on television.

Suddenly Mrs Tamm called up the stairs from the

hall.

'Letter for you, Lucy. It's on the hall table.'

'Thank you, Tammy,' and Lucy Jane raced downstairs. She tore open the envelope and read the words: 'Well, Pixie, is it going to be you who will play Isabella or some silly girl from an acting school? Do something! From the person who hopes to be your "brother" in *The Russell Adventure*.'

Lucy Jane read through the letter again and again before rushing upstairs to her bedroom to hide it under her pillow. Then she did her ballet practice. But she couldn't keep the secret to herself any longer and went to tell Tammy about the letter.

As she arrived in the kitchen the telephone rang, and Mrs Tamm went to answer it. Lucy Jane was gazing out of the window waiting to pass on the news when she noticed a pony and trap making its way up the drive. Sitting on the cart and holding the reins was Angela, wearing a little peaked cap that covered her cropped hair.

'Hello, Lucy,' she shouted to her from her little seat. 'Coming for a ride?'

'Ooh,' Lucy Jane replied excitedly, 'I'd love to but I'm supposed to be going to Glasgow with Granny.' She looked at Tammy, who was still on the telephone, and Mrs Tamm put her hand over the receiver and said, 'Run along with Angela. Don't be long. Just to the end of the drive and back. I'll call you when Mrs Mackenzie wants to leave.'

And with a very serious expression on her face, Mrs Tamm returned to her conversation, which she was obviously having great difficulty in hearing.

So Lucy Jane skipped out into the sunlit drive to join Angela.

'Lovely,' Lucy Jane said as she reached Angela and hopped into the cart.

They had only just started off when Lucy Jane heard Mrs Tamm calling, 'Come back quickly, Lucy. I think it's you that's wanted on the phone after all.'

But by the time Lucy Jane had climbed down from the cart Mrs Tamm was standing at the front door looking very agitated.

'I think it was a Mr Hall on the phone,' she said, 'but he couldn't hold on any longer so you'll have to wait until this evening. He said he wanted to speak to you urgently.'

'Mr Hall!' Lucy Jane exclaimed.

Angela turned excitedly to Lucy Jane.

'Maybe he wants you for the part,' Angela said. 'And now as you didn't speak to him you've lost it.'

Lucy Jane felt quite upset by Angela's remark and cross with herself for not coming to the phone as soon as Mrs Tamm had called her.

'Never mind,' Lucy Jane said as though she didn't care. 'Never mind, let's feed the horse.'

Just then the telephone rang again and Lucy Jane bounded back into the house to answer it. 'Maybe it's for me,' she shouted and she picked up the receiver.

'Lucy Jane speaking. Is that you, Mr Hall?'

'No, it's Mr McNee, the butcher. Is Mrs Mackenzie or Mrs Tamm at home?' the voice said.

'Yes,' Lucy Jane answered, disappointed. 'I'll get her,' and she called her grandmother. As she did so a black car screeched up the drive and Jack jumped out looking very worried and rushed to the front door.

'Lucy Jane,' he said. 'Lucy Jane, where's your mother?'

'In London.'

74

'Then who's in charge of you?' Jack asked, red in the face.

'My grandmother and Mrs Tamm,' Lucy Jane answered, putting her head right back to look at him, he was so tall.

'Then find them quickly,' he demanded.

Lucy Jane nodded and rushed to find her grandmother, who was still talking to the butcher. Angela waited in the drive holding on to the horse.

Mrs Mackenzie hurried into the hall, scratching her brow.

'What's all the fuss about? Who wants me?' she asked.

'It's Jack,' Lucy Jane said. 'You know, Jack from Star Television Films.'

'Can I help you? What is it?' she enquired as politely as she could.

'We need Lucy Jane in the film urgently. There's no time to explain now – but both Mr Hall and Mr Savage, the producer, tried to telephone you earlier. Mr Savage will come and see you after lunch,' Jack replied, still looking very flustered and worried.

'Well, surely everyone can wait until I've spoken to her parents and Mr Savage this afternoon,' Mrs Mackenzie protested, trying to calm Jack the best she could.

'Please, madam,' Jack pleaded, 'we must film this shot today. It's not much more than the back of her head again, but it's vitally important. There's no wig for Angela and we can't find another girl. Please!'

'Your shirt's undone,' Mrs Mackenzie said.

'Yes, sorry,' he answered flustered, 'but can we take Lucy Jane now? You see the scene HAS to be shot when the geese fly from the lake, they only settle once a year, and the geese have just settled on the lake, and,' he drew breath, 'we must film the children escaping from the castle with the geese flying in the background TODAY. Please, madam,' he implored.

'Well,' Mrs Mackenzie answered, bewildered, 'I suppose it's all right, as long as she's back in two hours. But,' Mrs Mackenzie continued, 'I'm worried, as I can't come with her because I'm waiting for a very important telephone call in half an hour and I must be here. And then we're going to Glasgow. But if you promise that Lucy Jane will be back in two hours and it's just for today, that's quite all right with me. We'll leave for Glasgow later, Lucy,' she added.

Jack looked relieved and immediately took Lucy Jane by the arm and bundled her into the back seat of the car. He slammed the door, jumped into the driving-seat and drove away at great speed before Lucy Jane had time to say a word to Angela or her grandmother.

Before she could ask what was happening they arrived at the castle and Joan, who was waiting for her, opened the car door and pulled her out and dragged her towards the caravan.

'Quick, into the caravan. I'll do your hair,' she puffed, then thrust a sheet of paper into Lucy Jane's hand. 'Learn this while I put in the rollers.' Lucy Jane's glasses steamed up with the excitement.

'What's happening?' Lucy Jane blurted out.

'You're playing Isabella today,' Joan said abruptly. 'I've got to get you ready as quick as I can, because the black geese have settled on the lake and they only do that once a year. Now is the only time the director can get the shot of the geese and Isabella, that's YOU, running away from the lake at the same time.'

'I understand,' Lucy Jane said, not understanding at

all. She looked at the piece of paper in her hand. Luckily she could read it despite the fact that she had taken off her glasses. The idea that she had to learn words she had never seen before so quickly made her nervous.

Suddenly the director burst into the caravan. 'Quick, get her into her clothes. Don't worry about her make-up or hair. It's a long shot, the camera will be far away. Quickly. The geese look restless and about to move. Come on. Fly, Lucy Jane, else we'll miss the shot.' And he left as abruptly as he had appeared. Lucy Jane bounced up from the chair and scampered as fast as she could into the wardrobe caravan followed by Joan.

'Thomasina, dress her quickly. The geese are about to move off the lake – we've got to get this shot before they do,' Joan said, and pushed Lucy Jane into Thomasina's arms, who stuffed her into the dress and coat as though she was a doll and then bundled her out through the caravan door again. Everyone seemed to be racing in different directions, including Jack who rushed over and grabbed Lucy Jane by the hand and started running with her towards the lake.

'My lines, my lines,' Lucy Jane screamed as she neared the water. 'Where are my lines?'

'Don't worry about that, just get in front of the camera and do what the director says,' he said, pushing Lucy Jane into Mr Hall's arms.

'Sorry about this,' the director said. 'Come with me and I'll show you what I want you to do.'

Lucy Jane nodded; as she looked up Andy was standing at the water's edge, watching her.

Then the director said, 'Hold these,' and handed her a large red carpet-bag and a rolled up blanket tied with a leather strap holding together the blanket and an old teddy bear made of worn brown velvet. 'When I say

"Action", run towards Daniel, you know, Andy, and say the words, "Quickly, Daniel, take these, quickly, they're following me," as though you are being chased by your uncle and his evil friends.'

Lucy Jane nodded again and repeated the words, 'Quickly, Daniel, take these, quickly, they're following me,' several times to herself.

The next moment the director shouted the words, 'Action, please,' and she started to run towards Daniel. She didn't have time to feel nervous but the cases felt heavy and her long petticoat kept tripping her up. Before she could remember what she had to say she tripped and fell, her arms spread-eagled, and the carpet-bag and the blanket bundle flew to either side of her. She picked herself up feeling very silly and tried to carry on running towards Andy who rushed over to help her. As he approached her he whispered, 'Say your lines, say your lines.'

Lucy Jane couldn't remember her lines and the only words that came into her head were, 'Quickly, Daniel,' so she repeated them twice and dusted herself down mumbling, 'Help me.' Then she looked round desperately to see if the director was cross as she wasn't sure if she should continue. His voice shouted, 'Cut. Cut. Fine. Move in for a close up. Quickly, while the geese are still there.' His words echoed across the lake. Lucy Jane staggered towards him. She looked so small carrying the huge bags that the director felt quite sorry for her.

'I'm sorry,' she stammered. 'I couldn't remember what I was supposed to say and the cases were so heavy I fell.'

To her surprise, he said kindly, 'Don't worry about that, we'll shoot the words again in a close up. We just needed the whole picture of you running with the geese

in the background. Now we must film your close up. All you have to do is remember what the lines mean.'

Lucy Jane looked up at him with her big round eyes.

'You know, remember that you are running away and *why*, and what you have to say is very urgent, otherwise your brother . . . ' The director stopped and looked at her. Then he squeezed her hand. 'Are you all right,

Lucy?' he asked, smiling. He called 'Make-up,' and immediately Joan was at his side.

'Give Lucy some sweat and untidy her hair, please, as I want her to look worn out and messy. As quick as you can, while the camera is still being set up.'

'Fine,' Joan said, and got out her big oblong fisherman's tackle box filled with make-up sponges and brushes and a selection of every colour of lipstick, eye shadow and skin foundation under the sun.

'Tina,' she called to her assistant. 'Mess up Lucy's hair while I dirty her cheeks and put some sweat on her face.'

The two ladies started working while Lucy Jane stood motionless as moist sponges and hair brushes came at her from all directions.

'Why didn't I look like this the last time?' she asked sensibly.

'Because the camera was so far away all it could see was the dot of a figure of a little girl and the black geese on the lake.' When Joan had finished she held up the glass and said, 'Like it? What do you think?'

Lucy Jane gasped. Her face was covered in black smudges, and little blobs of glycerine that looked like perspiration were dotted across her forehead. Her hair was matted and Tina had put twigs and leaves in it to make it look even more dishevelled.

'What do you think?' Joan asked again.

Lucy Jane thought she looked a mess, but she decided that if people were paid to make people look a mess and the director didn't see anything wrong in it, it was best to say nothing at all. But she thought it was ridiculous to make someone look such a fright, and all the magic of acting in front of a camera disappeared until Jack remarked, 'You look terrific, Lucy Jane, just like a real actress.'

Lucy Jane's heart swelled with pride and she turned to the director so he could see how she looked.

'Perfect. Just right, Lucy. Now then,' he said, 'I want you to say the same words again. But this time the camera will be much closer to your face.'

'Yes,' Lucy Jane answered quietly, her head filled with the joy of feeling like a proper actress.

'But,' he added, 'don't be put off if you see someone waving a sheet in the background to make the geese fly off the lake.'

Lucy Jane nodded.

'Now, come on, Lucy, let's rehearse.'

When she had rehearsed the scene twice, Mr Hall said, 'Good, now we'll go for a take.'

Jack called for silence and then the director whispered, 'Action, Lucy.'

So Lucy Jane said her lines again, but they didn't come out quite as she had expected, and the director cried, 'Cut. Cut. What's the matter, Lucy?'

Lucy didn't know, and now she was frightened as she thought the director looked so cross.

'We're going to do another take, Lucy,' he said as he walked over to her. 'Do it again, but this time be a little more worried, as though someone wicked is really following you, and try to remember the lines.' And he walked away without even a smile.

'All right,' she answered, thinking, 'I'll show the bad-tempered old toad,' and she started to jump up and down to make herself feel as if she had really been running away from someone.

Joan turned to Tina and whispered, 'She's a natural. No one has to tell her how to make herself out of breath. And the poor kid was just thrown into it.'

81

Tina nodded her head. The cameraman checked the camera while the assistant cried, 'Silence, everyone.' Then John Hall called softly, 'Now, action, Lucy.'

Lucy Jane immediately pretended to be terrified and called to her brother.

The director watched her intently. He was so proud that his new little star was so good and could be such a splendid actress at a moment's notice.

This time Lucy Jane didn't make any mistakes and was relieved when she heard, 'Good, Lucy, cut,' and saw the director walking over to her. 'Well done, Lucy,' he said. 'Very well done indeed.' He looked very pleased. 'That's all you need to do today,' and he smiled broadly and chucked Lucy Jane under the chin.

Lucy Jane felt very happy. She felt that at last she had really been in the film. Whether or not acting would become as important to her as dancing, she was yet to discover. But now she skipped around giddy with a new happiness she longed to share with her family.

8

Granny is Angry

Lucy Jane was feeling really warm inside. As she stood next to Mr Hall, who was sipping tea from a paper cup and discussing with the cameraman the next scene to be filmed, he asked her, 'Lucy, dear, do you want something to eat before you go?' and she felt at last the director really thought of her as part of the television crew. She was just about to answer when she saw her grandmother hurrying towards them looking extremely upset. Lucy Jane immediately felt worried. When Mrs Mackenzie arrived she was quite exhausted, but managed to say, 'I thought I said to bring Lucy Jane back in two hours. We've got to go to Glasgow.'

No one answered. Everyone looked at Mrs Mackenzie, amazed, most of all Lucy Jane, who had never seen her grandmother looking so fierce.

'I didn't say Lucy Jane could stay all day. You promised to bring her home. I insist that she leaves with me immediately.'

John Hall stepped forward and tried to pacify Mrs Mackenzie.

'Now, now,' he started in an even voice. 'Let's not get upset. It's all my fault.'

This patronizing tone upset Mrs Mackenzie even more.

'I have been extremely worried. I have been standing over there trying to come over and talk to you for nearly an hour,' she said. 'And some man who called himself a production supervisor refused to let me.'

Lucy Jane felt embarrassed. Her grandmother was making her look like a baby in front of everyone.

'Please, Granny, don't be cross,' Lucy Jane said, trying to calm her grandmother, and feeling tears coming to her eyes. 'I don't know why you're so upset, Granny. You said I could go and I know Mummy will be happy when she hears I'm going to be on television.'

'Your mother will be as cross as I am,' Mrs Mackenzie retorted, annoyed by Lucy Jane's impertinence. 'Especially when she knows you have been whisked out of the house and worked hours longer than promised without so much as a *contract* or *proper agreement*. That's the bit that annoys me. I've been worried out of my mind. No one in an official capacity has been to see me about this. No one. You could have been kidnapped.' She finished, still looking extremely agitated.

At that moment, a very harassed and hot-looking Mr Savage came hurrying down the hill. His suit, which was normally well pressed, looked quite crushed, as did his face. His tie and hair were hanging to one side.

'Ah, here is our producer Mr Savage!'

'John! John!' Mr Savage puffed as he finally arrived at the little group. 'I couldn't find the Mackenzie farmhouse, so I haven't seen the grandmother or

85

explained anything to her and to crown it all the car had a puncture,' he went on, looking most concerned.

Someone immediately brought Mr Savage a chair and Mr Hall signalled for another chair to be brought for Mrs Mackenzie.

'I'm so sorry about all this. Sit down, dear lady,' Mr Hall said, offering Mrs Mackenzie a chair.

'I have no intention of sitting down until this matter is settled,' said Mrs Mackenzie.

Mr Savage stepped forward.

'Madam!' he said. 'So you are Mrs Mackenzie! I have been looking for you everywhere.'

Mrs Mackenzie raised her eyebrows.

'I am Marty Savage, the producer,' he said politely.

'I hope you are nothing like your name,' Mrs Mackenzie answered, looking straight at him.

'As the producer, I am to blame. Please do me the honour of letting me apologise. I must explain and sort everything out with you. Would you join me for dinner at my hotel tonight? Then we can discuss the whole matter.'

Lucy Jane prayed that her grandmother would say 'Yes'.

'Well,' Mrs Mackenzie said finally, 'I think it is all pretty shabby, but we have to talk and tonight is as good a time as any.'

Lucy Jane was relieved. She bit her lip, hoping that her cheeks had not gone red.

Mrs Mackenzie looked at her and said, 'Look at you, dearie, what have they done to you?'

'They made me an actress,' Lucy Jane said meekly, trying to stop the tears.

'Actress!' her grandmother exclaimed. 'Poor darling, you look a fright.' And with that she took Lucy Jane by the hand and marched her up the hill to the caravan to change, saying, 'You've really blotted your copybook, my girl.'

As Lucy Jane walked towards the caravan she noticed Andy in his shirt-sleeves leaning against the door, eating an apple.

'Coming to rushes tomorrow?' he asked as though nothing had happened.

Lucy cast her eyes to the ground. She struggled to hold up her petticoats and skirt so that they wouldn't get dirty and hoped he couldn't notice she was about to cry.

'What are "rushes"?' Lucy Jane asked, still not looking up.

'Rushes,' Andy explained, 'are when they show the work filmed the day before. They "rush" the film through!'

'I'd like to,' Lucy Jane replied, 'but I don't want to copy my blotty book.'

Andy laughed. 'You mean blot your copybook, Pixie.'

Lucy Jane was so annoyed with herself that she didn't answer.

'You could come and see the rushes tonight,' Andy said. 'But you won't be in them, of course, as they're a day behind. So come tomorrow and see yourself on screen. If your grandmother lets you.' He paused, grinning at her. 'What do you think, Pixie?'

Lucy Jane could see her grandmother was still furious, so without answering she went quickly into the caravan to change.

When they arrived at the farmhouse after a silent journey Chris handed Mrs Mackenzie two envelopes.

'These are the documents Mr Savage tried to deliver to you this afternoon,' he said politely. 'Mr Savage's car

87

will collect you at seven, Mrs Mackenzie.'

He smiled, slid back into the driver's seat and drove away.

As soon as they were inside the house Lucy Jane forgot all the fuss and asked excitedly, 'What's in the envelopes, Granny? Please let's see!' and she skipped around the room.

Mrs Mackenzie replied, 'I'm exhausted and not up to doing anything until I've had my cup of tea. I was so worried about you, darling,' she said.

Suddenly Lucy Jane felt sorry for her granny and she went up and squeezed her hand. She looked up at her and said, 'Don't worry. It's all over now.'

Mrs Tamm brought the tea into the sitting room and placed the tray on a small table next to Mrs Mackenzie's favourite chair.

Lucy Jane waited patiently while Mrs Mackenzie finished her second cup of tea, then asked anxiously, 'Can we open the envelopes now, Granny?'

'No, dearie, not at the moment,' her grandmother said. 'I must ring my friend in Glasgow and explain what happened. Then I have to change for dinner. I'll open them when I'm ready,' and she rose from her chair and went to the phone.

When Mrs Mackenzie came downstairs she was in quite a cheerful frame of mind and said, 'We'll go to Glasgow another day, dearie. Now I think I'll have a glass of sherry,' and she pushed her hair into place and checked her lipstick in the mirror over the mantelpiece.

'Lucy, darling,' she said, as she finished her sherry. 'Bring me those envelopes and then fetch my glasses and we'll see what Star Television Films have to say.'

Lucy Jane was overjoyed. She polished her own glasses, and stood eagerly by her grandmother.

Suddenly the telephone rang and Mrs Mackenzie put the letters aside.

'Rats,' Lucy Jane thought as she took off her glasses.

At that moment her grandmother called her.

'Lucy, darling, it's your mother,' she said.

Lucy Jane bounced across the room to the telephone. 'What shall I tell her?' Lucy Jane asked her urgently.

'Just tell her the truth,' her grandmother said calmly. 'And I'll telephone her later to sort out everything.'

Lucy Jane was so happy to hear her mother's voice that she almost forgot about the film and just chatted away.

'How many days until you arrive, Mummy?' she asked suddenly. She was just about to replace the receiver when she whispered, 'Mummy, I've got something to tell you.' There was a long pause while Lucy Jane looked round to see if anyone was listening. 'Granny got very cross today, she even . . . ' She stopped abruptly as her grandmother came into the room.

'Here's Granny,' she said quickly and handed the receiver to her grandmother.

She waited for her granny to open the envelopes but alas, before she could do so, the car arrived to take her grandmother to dinner and the envelopes remained unopened.

That night Lucy Jane lay awake as long as she could, hoping to hear the news when her grandmother returned. But Mrs Mackenzie was so late that Lucy Jane had already fallen asleep.

The next day, breakfast seemed to last for ever and Mrs Mackenzie talked about everything under the sun, except the film. Finally the suspense was so great that Lucy Jane jumped to her feet, picked up her piece of toast from her plate and threw it out of the window saying, 'That will give the birds something to eat and they can eat the envelopes too!' Then she burst into tears and ran from the room and upstairs as fast as she could, slamming the door behind her.

Mrs Mackenzie calmly rose from the table and followed Lucy Jane upstairs. Lucy Jane was so upset she had locked herself in her room and put a chair in front of the door, so no one could get in.

'Now stop this nonsense,' Mrs Mackenzie said sternly. 'I have the envelopes and I won't tell you what's in them unless you come out here at once.'

There was a very long silence and then slowly and quietly Lucy Jane turned the handle and her small tear-stained face appeared round the side of the door.

'Now come out here at once and apologise,' her grandmother said firmly.

Lucy Jane didn't want to apologise.

'Sorry for throwing the toast,' Lucy Jane said quietly and went back inside the room. But this time she didn't close the door. She just went and sat on her bed, buried her face in her tickly rug and cried and cried.

Mrs Mackenzie felt a little sorry for her, but she remained firm and said sternly, 'I'll be downstairs in the sitting room when you're ready to come and talk sensibly,' and went downstairs without another word.

Lucy Jane could hardly hear what her granny was saying, she was sobbing so loudly, partly from the frustration of her grandmother's indifference to the television film, and partly because she was cross with herself for losing her temper.

'Now I've really copied my blotty book or blotted my copybook,' she thought and started to cry even more loudly. Her cheeks were hot, her lips were quivering and she couldn't stop the tears splashing from her eyes. She lay like this for some time, wondering if she would ever know what was in the letters. She hoped her grandmother wouldn't tell her mother she had behaved so badly, but more important, she hoped her grandmother would not forbid her to be in the film.

9

The Joke That Goes Wrong

When Lucy Jane had stopped crying she dried her eyes, washed her face and reluctantly ventured into the sitting room. Mrs Mackenzie looked up over her glasses and said gently, 'Sit down, dearie. Now,' she continued firmly, 'no more nonsense and we'll go through the envelopes together. The first one is for you,' and she handed Lucy Jane a large brown envelope marked 'MISS LUCY JANE TADWORTH'. Lucy Jane took the envelope and opened it nervously. Inside was the script of the television film with Lucy Jane's name on it. She held it to her chest for a moment. 'Mine,' she gasped and smiled to herself, feeling a little lump at the back of her throat.

Then Mrs Mackenzie opened the next envelope which was filled with several sheets of paper and two letters.

'My word,' Mrs Mackenzie exclaimed. 'Better go through these slowly and see what they say. Can you fetch my other glasses, Lucy? The print is so small.'

Lucy Jane bounced up, skipped across the room and collected her grandmother's glasses and then she cleaned her own. When she returned she leant on her granny's shoulder and put her arm round her neck, her fingers curling into her granny's hair, happy that at last they were opening the letters together. 'Now, let's see,' Mrs Mackenzie said, and they started to go through the sheets of paper.

Lucy Jane was so excited she felt as though fireworks were going off in her head and she jumped up, kissed the cat, then her granny and was about to rush out and kiss Mrs Tamm when her grandmother called her.

'Come on, Lucy dearie, let's look at the rest.' So obediently Lucy Jane came back and snuggled up to her grandmother.

The next pieces of paper were all very official-looking. First was a long letter to Mrs Tadworth and Mrs Mackenzie asking Mrs Mackenzie to sign the enclosed contract so that Lucy Jane could be in the television film. They also wanted to know if Mrs Mackenzie would be Lucy Jane's chaperone, for which she would be paid. If not, the television company would provide a lady to look after Lucy Jane. Next was the contract, in which Lucy Jane was to be contracted for three weeks to play the part of Isabella – providing she did not cut her hair until the filming was finished.

Now at last Lucy Jane really *knew* she was in the film – there was a piece of paper to prove it, and after all the frustration and confusion, she felt really happy.

'Tell me, Granny,' she said excitedly as she leant over her grandmother's shoulder and gave her a hug. 'What words do I have to say tomorrow?'

'Well, let's look it up. It says page 37/38,' her grandmother replied. They turned over the pages of the script.

When Lucy Jane saw the word 'Nursery' she thought it must be the part she had filmed when only the back of her head was showing.

'That was the day Angela cut off all her hair and I stood in for her. Look, this is my part,' Lucy Jane said, pointing to the page. She took off her glasses, and looked at her grandmother.

The expression on her face was a very special one. Mrs Mackenzie was pleased to see Lucy Jane looking so happy at last. She had been really worried until Lucy Jane's mother had said that she would be delighted for Lucy Jane to be in the television film if they asked her.

She took Lucy Jane's hands, looked at her warmly and asked, 'Do you need me to help you, Lucy?'

'No, thank you, Granny,' she answered, feeling very grown-up and standing as tall as she could. 'I'll learn the lines and when I think I know them, maybe you can help me,' she said, and skipped towards the door. She was elated by her granny's change of heart and had a happy feeling inside now that she and her granny were really friends again.

'Good,' said her grandmother, rising from her chair and folding up the contract and the letter. 'Good,' she repeated, happy now too.

The next day after breakfast, Lucy Jane said to her grandmother excitedly, 'I think I've learned my lines, so I'm going to read the whole script before I go to work.'

'All right, dearie,' Mrs Mackenzie said as she folded her napkin. 'I've got to take Mrs Tamm urgently to the dentist. But Mary is here until you go so you won't be alone.' She was just about to leave when she bent down and kissed Lucy Jane and added, 'By the way, they have a nice chaperone for you – Nancy Notts. I think it's best she does it, as I wouldn't know what to do. Also I must be here when Jeremy and Mummy and Daddy arrive.'

'That's all right,' Lucy Jane agreed, pleased that her granny would be at home to welcome her parents and her brother. She ran up to her bedroom, sat on the end of the bed, cleaned her glasses and started to read the script. No sooner had she settled into the story than she heard clippity-clop on the drive and she knew it must be Angela coming to visit her.

'Anyone at home?' Angela called from below. Lucy Jane ran to her bedroom window; the sun was shining, the trees lining the drive were waving in the wind and she could just see Angela between the leaves, standing in the cart holding the reins.

Lucy Jane wondered if Angela would be upset now she was really going to play the part. Not sure what to do, Lucy Jane decided it was best to go down.

'I'm coming!' Lucy Jane shouted out of the window and ran downstairs. When she arrived at the front door Angela was still standing in the cart and greeted her with, 'Hello, Goodie Two Shoes.'

'Hello,' Lucy Jane replied, giving her a welcoming smile.

'Do you want a ride?'

'No, thank you. Well, I mean, yes please, but I have got some learning to do.'

'You definitely going to play my part, then?' Angela asked, a wistful tone entering her voice, a tone Lucy Jane had never heard before.

'Well, yes, I think I am,' Lucy Jane replied sheepishly, not really wanting to admit to Angela that she had now officially taken her part.

'Oh, wonderful!' Angela beamed joyfully. 'Wonderful, I hoped they'd choose you.' And she jumped up and down as though this was the best news in the world.

'Thanks, Coconut-head.' Lucy Jane was grateful that Angela had been such a sport about it. 'But,' she added, 'I think I ought to stay here and read the script.' Lucy Jane looked very serious.

'Oh, rubbish! I didn't bother with the script . . . Can't read properly anyway,' and she laughed.

'And look what happened!' Lucy Jane replied. 'Jumping cactus, you didn't know you shouldn't cut off your hair. And you were first choice,' Lucy Jane added emphatically.

'Well, I didn't know that I shouldn't, you see, Orange Pips. Hadn't read the story,' and she scratched her cropped head of hair.

Lucy Jane looked at her, and then started to climb up into the apple tree. Angela followed. When they had settled on a large branch Lucy Jane looked up from her script and asked, 'Are you . . . ' She stopped, then choosing her words carefully said, 'Do you have trouble reading, then? Is that why you can't read?' Lucy Jane asked seriously.

'Think so,' Angela replied, confused. 'You see, my teacher has only just discovered what the problem is, so now I go to Glasgow for special lessons once a week because I've got some foreign word like diesexy wrong with me. That means 'can't read'. Don't worry,' Angela assured her, 'it's not catching.'

'That's strange. You can't read, and I need to wear glasses. Now I know you can't read, I don't mind wearing glasses!' Lucy Jane laughed good-naturedly. 'Is that why your mother needs the television money? For your extra lessons. For your diesexy?' Lucy Jane asked concerned, then she added, 'But isn't it called dislexie? "Diesexy" sounds rather rude.'

'Think so, Orange Pips,' Angela replied, laughing.

They were engrossed in the story some time later when suddenly they heard a car honking its horn in the drive.

'Lucy Jane, it's time to leave for work,' Chris, one of the assistants, called.

'I'll come with you,' Angela enthused as she started climbing down from the tree. Lucy Jane didn't reply and she carefully made her way down through the branches.

'Come on, quickly, Lucy,' Angela called impatiently to Lucy Jane as she jumped to the ground.

'I don't want to fall,' Lucy Jane called back, and gingerly continued to make her descent.

'Oh, peanuts,' Angela replied. 'You are a silly,' Angela said, bounding up the tree again. 'Look,' she said to Lucy, who at last had reached the bottom. 'Watch this,' and she scooted down the tree at great speed, landing with a huge jump.

'That was brilliant,' Lucy Jane exclaimed enthusiastically, not noticing that Angela was huddled up in pain and hugging her toes.

'Oh, custard pie, I think I've gone and broken my foot,' Angela said matter-of-factly.

'Oh, I hope not,' Lucy Jane said, bending over to her friend, concerned.

Sure enough, Angela was in such pain she couldn't walk and Chris had to rush over to help her to her feet. He called to Mrs Mackenzie whose car at that moment was making its way up the drive. She stopped the car and walked over to Angela, and bent down to look at the child's foot.

'Oh, dear, dear!' she puffed, as Angela cried in pain. 'I'll have to take you to the doctor.' Mrs Mackenzie looked very worried. 'Lucy, you'd better go and do your filming otherwise you'll be late,' she added.

So Lucy Jane gave a quick wave and ran towards the car, leaving her grandmother to take care of Angela.

When Lucy Jane arrived at the castle Andy was standing in front of the make-up caravan waving his arms and shouting.

'Welcome, Pixie!'

'Do we have chaperones?' Lucy Jane asked.

'Yes. *Dragons!*' Andy answered bluntly.

Lucy Jane immediately skipped over to the caravan to be made-up, delighted that she was about to start work on her first official day. She settled into the chair and Joan asked amiably, 'How are you this morning?'

'Very well, thank you,' Lucy Jane replied. She was feeling quite nervous, but she decided not to mention that. 'And how are you, Joan?' she asked in the most casual and relaxed tone she could.

'A little tired, but well enough, thank you.' Then she added, 'Know your lines?'

'Yes, I think so.'

'Good,' she said and finished getting Lucy Jane ready. 'Now, run along,' and she hurried Lucy Jane out of the door to go and change her clothes. Dressing up was one of the things Lucy Jane liked best.

As it was the continuation of the nursery scene, Lucy Jane had to wear the same frock with the blue and white gingham pinafore she wore on the first day. But luckily the petticoat, bodice and shoes all seemed much more comfortable than before. Although it wasn't an especially pretty costume Lucy Jane loved wearing the long skirts and frilly petticoats.

When she was ready she cried out, 'Oh, jumping cactus – Angela!' At that moment she heard a voice calling behind her. It was her grandmother.

'I've brought Angela to see you. She's down the hill in the car.'

Angela was sitting on the bonnet of the car grinning from ear to ear, her leg held high, displaying her bandaged foot.

'Think I've broken all me toes,' Angela smiled and fell back on to the bonnet laughing, which made Lucy Jane laugh as well. 'My mother's going to have a fit,' Angela said merrily.

'I don't blame her,' Lucy Jane answered sagely. 'You're a wildcat,' and she went over to help Angela slide off the car.

'Can't stay long,' Lucy Jane said, 'as they'll need me soon. But maybe you can come to tea at the weekend?'

'That would be chocolate cake,' Angela replied, and Lucy Jane skipped away to start her first proper day's filming.

The following week Angela came to visit Lucy Jane on the set again. Suddenly she whispered something into Lucy Jane's ear. The two girls made their way unsteadily over to the make-up caravan. Angela's foot was still bandaged and she was limping and leaning heavily on Lucy Jane.

'Oh, Joan is so fussy,' Angela said as they struggled up the steps into the caravan. 'This will be really good fun,' she continued happily as she closed the caravan door. 'And give them a big laugh as I think you've been too good for too long.'

Inside Joan's caravan the girls could be heard laughing and chatting non-stop.

Twenty minutes later a very agitated assistant arrived looking for Lucy Jane to start work and rapped on the door.

'Are you in there, Lucy Jane?' he called out, concerned.

'Won't be long,' Lucy Jane replied, and giggled.

More giggles. Then silence.

'Quickly, they're waiting for you,' and he opened the caravan door.

'Oh, my God!' he exclaimed as he saw Lucy Jane standing there with a huge red mark on one side of her face, her teeth blacked out with eyebrow pencil and her foot and arm bandaged up to the size of a football.

'Oh, blimey!' he said. 'What have you been up to?'

The girls didn't answer, just looked at each other and fell on to one another's shoulders, giggling.

'The Gov'nor will go barmy when he sees you,' he exclaimed nervously and ran up the hill to fetch the director and Joan.

Lucy Jane and Angela waited on the steps, still laughing. Lucy Jane looked very strange grinning from ear to ear with her blacked-out teeth, and Angela didn't look much better with a bit of pink ribbon on her chopped-off hair and a bandaged foot. They looked up the hill and saw John Hall and Joan rushing towards them.

When he saw Lucy Jane, the director cried out, 'Oh no. This is ridiculous.' He was ashen with rage.

'Oh, no, this is a joke,' Lucy Jane replied seriously.

'A very bad one,' Joan answered primly. 'Time is money. You're wasting time and therefore money.'

The director gave Joan a sharp look and said, 'I'll deal with this,' and pushed past Joan to talk to the girls.

'Lucy, how could you be so silly?' he said. 'Now, get ready at once. Although this is not a very long part,' he added, 'it is a very important one and could make any little girl who plays it into a star. How could you throw away a chance like this? If my daughter was old enough she could play it and I'd make her a star,' Mr Hall finished angrily.

Then he noticed both Angela's and Lucy Jane's bandaged feet, and he went quite white.

'What's this? Which foot is really broken?' he enquired, worried that his new star would not be able to walk. The girls started to laugh again.

'Angela's,' Lucy Jane giggled, and waved her foot in the air.

'This is no laughing matter,' Mr Hall said. 'Undo those bandages immediately.' And he walked away, leaving Joan to sort out the mess. Neither Lucy Jane nor Angela could understand why the director hadn't enjoyed their joke and they both looked rather disappointed.

'Now then, out of here,' Joan said sternly to Angela. Angela hobbled out of the caravan, and Joan closed the door smartly behind her.

'Now, young lady,' she said, 'let's get you back into working order. You're a silly girl.'

Lucy Jane looked up at her, amazed that she too had taken the game so seriously.

'Clean that stuff off your teeth,' she said, handing Lucy Jane a Kleenex. Lucy Jane and Joan were in the caravan for some fifteen minutes before Lucy Jane emerged spotless and ready for work. Angela was still waiting outside. When Lucy Jane saw her she whispered, 'You'd better go home, wildcat. She's in a tiger-like rage.'

'OK,' Angela agreed and hobbled off down the hill.

'That girl!' Joan said, looking at her. 'She's nothing but trouble and you'd do a lot better if you kept well away from her.'

'I like her,' Lucy Jane replied boldly. 'Anyway,' she added, 'if a dandelion does something silly, why blame the leaf?'

Joan had no idea what she meant and she firmly took hold of Lucy Jane's hand and hurried her up the hill to work.

10

Lucy Jane Gets a Shock

Lucy Jane was sitting meekly in the caravan at lunchtime waiting to be called when there was a sharp rap at the door and a voice said, 'Rushes, Joan. In the school hall. One o'clock.'

'Thanks,' Joan called back. Then she asked Lucy Jane, 'We're off to see rushes before lunch. You coming?'

'I don't know. Am I invited?' Lucy Jane asked apprehensively.

'I don't see why not, as long as you behave yourself,' she said, tidying the brushes on the dressing table. 'Follow me, young lady,' which Lucy Jane did.

When they arrived at the school hall, Jack told her, 'You're going to see yourself close up.'

Lucy Jane's stomach turned over. She didn't know what to expect and suddenly felt quite terrified.

Immediately everyone in the hall sat down and the lights were dimmed. On the big screen at the end of the hall were shots of the lake. Then there were shots of black geese and, suddenly, there was a shot of Lucy Jane. Lucy Jane running with the carpet-bag in the distance. Lucy Jane running and falling and calling to her brother. Lucy Jane's heart beat faster and faster as she saw more and more film of herself. The next picture on the screen was about twenty times bigger than life size. It was her own face covered in smudges, looking very hot with messy hair. Her face looked so huge that she wanted to cry, but she kept quiet. Then when she heard her own voice she put her hands over her ears as it sounded so strange and squeaky and she wished she could hide under the seat. But Joan was sitting next to her so she just lowered her head and covered her face with her hands and pretended she wasn't there.

To her embarrassment the whole scene was shown once more and Lucy Jane would have been happy if she could have fallen through the floorboards rather than watch herself again. She kept her head lowered and her ears covered, but she still heard her own voice and the cameraman saying:

'Excellent. Just what was wanted.'

Everyone mumbled in agreement and also commented on the perfection of the geese in the background. Lucy Jane also liked the geese but when Joan said, 'Wonderful, wonderful, those geese flying off the lake. Beautiful,' and the cameraman agreed, 'Couldn't be better,' Lucy Jane wondered if everyone thought the geese were better than she was. Maybe, she decided, it was because she had been so silly. Her worst fears were confirmed when the director added, 'Those geese make the shot. You don't notice anything else.' Lucy Jane was half relieved no one had noticed her.

At last the lights came up and the crew shuffled to

their feet and made their way back into their cars and drove back to the location for lunch, leaving Lucy Jane still standing alone in the hall.

When everyone was back at the castle for lunch, the director looked round anxiously and asked, 'Where's Lucy?' But Lucy Jane was nowhere to be found. Very concerned Mr Hall asked Jack, and Jack then asked Joan, 'Have you seen Lucy Jane?'

'No, I thought she came back with you.'

John Hall was now extremely worried.

Suddenly the whole crew were searching for Lucy Jane. Andy decided not to waste any more time and jumped on to a bicycle parked by one of the caravans and rode back to the village hall as quickly as he could. He thought Lucy Jane might have found the whole experience overwhelming but, on the other hand, she might still be waiting there for a lift.

When Andy arrived at the school hall it was completely empty.

'Lucy Jane,' he called, 'are you here?' He looked everywhere but couldn't find her. Just as he was leaving he heard a muffled sound coming from behind a cupboard door. He went over to it and listened. Someone was in there. He opened the door and there, sitting huddled at the back of the cupboard amongst all the brooms, was Lucy Jane sobbing her heart out.

'Pixie, what's the matter?' Andy asked kindly. 'What's happened?' He lifted Lucy Jane's tear-stained face, and looked into her brown eyes which now looked very sore. 'Oh, Pixie,' he said. 'What is it?'

'I was so awful,' Lucy Jane sobbed. 'I looked so silly and my voice was so squeaky,' and again she hid her face in her hands and sobbed. Andy was not quite sure what he should do. He didn't have any sisters and he had

never seen anyone so upset before.

'Come on, Lucy. Better get back to the location,' he said, holding out his hand. But Lucy Jane just shook her head and was determined to stay huddled in the corner of the cupboard amid the brooms, buckets and mops.

'I'll go and fetch the director,' Andy thought to himself, and he ran outside into the warm sun again and jumped on to his bicycle and made his way back to the castle. When he arrived Mr Hall was still frantically searching for Lucy Jane. He was just about to get into his car and go to Lucy Jane's home before contacting the police when Andy shouted, 'She's in the broom cupboard at the school. She's very upset.'

'Thank heaven you've found her,' the director replied and immediately drove to the hall.

'Lucy, darling!' he said. 'What on earth's the matter?'

'I looked so silly, and sounded so squeaky, my face is so awful and I don't want to act any more,' she continued to sob.

The director had never come across this behaviour before, and although he had a daughter of his own he was rather puzzled that she was making such a fuss. But nevertheless he put his arms round her and wiped her eyes, saying, 'Now come on, Lucy. Don't be upset, you were supposed to do everything you did and your acting looked and sounded just right.'

And he gave her another squeeze and led her gently back to the car. She was silent all the way to the castle and all that afternoon Lucy Jane remained very quiet. Only Andy and the director knew the truth about the upset, so Mr Hall decided that it was best if Sandra Woods, who played the children's servant in the film, stayed with her that afternoon instead of Nancy Notts, the chaperone, who was often agitated and would keep asking Lucy Jane why she had sore, red eyes.

Although Lucy Jane was feeling quite despondent, she was professional and well-behaved the whole afternoon, and grateful that Miss Woods was more relaxed than Nancy, who was constantly asking Lucy Jane and Andy if they had washed their hands. 'Go to the toilet and don't forget to wash your hands,' she would say every time there was a break.

Andy had pulled Lucy Jane to one side and warned

her, 'Take no notice if Nancy comes over to you. If you don't want to go to the lavatory, don't bother. She thinks we're babies.' He stopped and looked at her. 'You probably *are* a baby after the way you behaved today,' he said, teasing her. And walked away, laughing.

Lucy Jane was furious, and wanted to cry, but she called after him, saying, 'And you are damned annoying,' and stormed off in the opposite direction, hoping she would never see him again.

But when Lucy Jane arrived back at the farmhouse she still wasn't happy. So she went straight into the sitting room to see if her grandmother had arrived back from Glasgow.

But Mrs Mackenzie wasn't there so Lucy Jane decided to go and see Mrs Tamm instead. But as Mrs Tamm wasn't around either she sat on the stairs and thought of all that had happened to her since she had arrived in Scotland.

She remained on the stairs, a happy tingling feeling growing inside. When at last she skipped down into the hall she saw a car from Star Television Films driving up with a letter. Lucy Jane hurriedly opened the envelope. She studied the sheet carefully and read:

FRIDAY NIGHT CALL
Scene 21. Escape from the castle.
Then Lucy Jane looked down the page and saw her name marked.
Lucy Jane Tadworth. Make-up call 6.00 p.m.
'Friday! Two days away. I'm glad it's not tomorrow,' Lucy Jane thought as she looked at the piece of paper, relieved she would not have to face Andy and Mr Hall the following day.

'But a night call? Filming at NIGHT!' She could stay

up late! She could hardly wait. She regretted having ever thought of leaving.

'I think I'll stay in the television film,' she decided. 'Night filming sounds exciting. And as Mummy used to say, "Not everything in life is the way you want it to be."'

11

Night Call

'Night shooting' was yet another adventure that Lucy Jane was to discover. At six p.m. an assistant arrived and Lucy Jane was duly waiting, standing hugging her script to her chest.

When Lucy Jane arrived at the castle it all looked quite different. There was a thrilling atmosphere, and at last Lucy Jane really appreciated that being in this television film was a chance of a lifetime.

As she got out of the car Mr Savage was standing by the caravans waiting for her.

'Lucy Jane,' he said in a low voice. 'I'd like to speak to your father when we've finished filming.'

Lucy Jane looked worried.

'Are you angry, Mr Savage?' Lucy Jane asked, concerned.

'No,' Mr Savage continued, 'I have some news for him which I think will be quite a pleasant surprise.' And without further explanation he walked off, leaving Lucy

Jane wondering what on earth the surprise could possibly be.

As she ran to the caravan to get ready the crew called out, 'Hello, Lucy love. How's our little "sweetie squeaky" tonight?'

Lucy Jane thought it was lovely that everyone was so friendly and pleased to see her.

'Hello, Jack, hello, Dave,' she called as she skipped between the members of the crew towering over her.

Then she noticed behind the crew three trestle tables with lots of thermos flasks, hot-water bottles, blankets and extra coats laid out on them, and wondered what they were for.

She changed quickly and waited to be called. A few minutes later Jack collected her and they went to the north wing of the castle where the escape of the Russell children was to be filmed. She felt a little frightened at the thought of seeing Mr Hall again, but she was determined that from now on she would be sensible.

When she arrived at the castle, a cold wind started to howl and she thought how nice it would be to have the blankets and hot water bottles and wondered if she was supposed to have taken one.

Everyone seemed to be rushing about in all directions. There were carpenters erecting huge platforms on which to stand the lamps, and electricians hauling the huge lamps on to the platforms once they were ready.

Charlie the electrician said to his mate, 'You think those brutes are safe in this wind, Dave?'

'Sure,' Dave replied and moved off to start getting the smaller lamps in position.

Lucy Jane stood patiently by her chaperone feeling a little cold despite her long clothes, petticoats and velvet coat. Suddenly someone shouted, 'Grips! Sparks! The lamp is falling,' and everyone started shouting and screaming as a gust of wind made the huge lamp standing on the platform topple to the ground.

Nancy Notts immediately started wailing hysterically, and dropped the chocolate and magazine she was holding.

Quick as lightning someone flung their arms round Lucy Jane and swept her to one side and on to the ground, crying, 'Careful, Pixie!'

When she looked up she found Andy holding her; he had saved her from the huge light still smouldering on the ground a few feet away.

At this moment John Hall rushed over to see if his two young stars had been injured. 'Oh, Lucy! Thank heavens,' he puffed as he arrived. 'Someone said you'd been hurt.'

Lucy Jane was so happy that Mr Hall was not cross that tears came to her eyes. When he lifted her into his arms and kissed her and said, 'There, there, Lucy darling,' she sobbed quietly on his shoulder, relieved that her foolishness had been forgotten.

Suddenly the first assistant shrieked, 'OK, chaps, quiet please, let's go for a rehearsal. Come on, kids.'

The two other young actors that Lucy Jane had only met once before walked over to her.

'Do you remember me? I play Clarissa, Isabella's sister,' the tall girl said politely, 'and this is Tony. He plays Alexander, our big brother.'

'How do you do?' Lucy Jane said, and held out her hand and looked up to the tall boy with dark hair. He looked about sixteen and very friendly. Annabelle, who played Clarissa, was very pretty with fair hair and violet eyes. She was tall and, although she was only thirteen,

113

Lucy Jane thought she seemed very grown up, and the way she smiled made Lucy Jane feel in awe of her.

Everyone shook hands and Mr Hall explained what he wanted them to do, once the moon was high in the sky.

'What I need you all to do is quite difficult. In the first shot,' he said, 'you will all be carrying your various bundles and animals and Lucy, you will have to carry a live duck as you escape from the castle, and you will have to try and run with wind and rain machines blowing against you.' Then the director smiled at everyone and hurried back to the camera.

While they waited to start work the children jumped up and down to keep warm, especially Lucy Jane, who thought that filming at night was even more special than filming in the day.

The moon made the castle look rather eerie, and the camera and lamps looked like strange robot people from out of space.

Then suddenly Jack herded them all with their dogs, bags, bundles and the duck, into position to film. They huddled against the castle wall; the girls in their long full skirts, velvet coats and bonnets and the boys in breeches and tweed jackets and flat caps made a charming picture.

Then Jack called, 'Action, wind machines! Action, rain!' and instantly Lucy Jane was nearly blown to the ground by the sudden gust of wind from the giant fans and the heavy rain produced by the fireman's hose blowing in her face.

The director shouted, 'Action, children!' and the dogs immediately started barking and the children found it hard to walk against the force of the wind and rain. Their feet kept slipping in the mud and the girls'

114

long skirts became heavy with water as the relentless wind forced their bodies backwards. Luckily Lucy Jane's duck seemed to like all the water splashing on its face, even if Lucy Jane didn't! But she didn't grumble and bravely kept hold of the quacking bird as she staggered forward acting her part very well.

'What a little trooper!' Mr Hall observed to the cameraman as they filmed Lucy Jane and the other children battling through the rain.

Suddenly Annabelle fell to the ground on top of her bundles, and Andy rushed forward to help her.

'I'm a small girl at heart,' she remarked sweetly as he gallantly helped her to her feet. 'But she pushed me,' Annabelle said, giving Lucy Jane a spiteful look.

Lucy Jane was furious and thought it served Annabelle right that she now looked ridiculous, covered in mud.

'Cut! Cut!' the director called, annoyed that Annabelle wasn't really trying and had spoilt the shot by pretending to fall.

As soon as they heard the word 'Cut', the make-up, wardrobe and hairdressing people rushed over to the children and wrapped towels and coats round them and gave them hot-water bottles, hot drinks and tried to dry their faces and hair.

'This is exciting,' Lucy Jane said as she hugged her hot-water bottle.

'Only to a beginner like you,' Annabelle replied sarcastically, water dripping on to her nose. 'We must be fools to get wet deliberately for Art,' she said, turning her back on Lucy Jane and smiling at Andy.

'She's really rude,' Lucy Jane thought, glad she had Angela as a friend.

When they had done the scene again Jack called,

'OK, boys and girls. That's it. Thank you. On to the next shot. Now, kids, go to the caravan and get warm.'

As they stood in the caravan holding hot-water bottles, warming themselves round the paraffin stove, there was a feeling of friendship and togetherness that made Lucy Jane feel happy inside and reminded her of the ballet.

Suddenly there was a bang at the caravan door and John Hall came in and announced, 'I don't think we're going to need you again tonight, Lucy, dear. It's past midnight and I think you should change to go home.'

'That's good,' Annabelle whispered to Andy. Luckily Lucy Jane didn't hear.

'When you've changed, I'd like to talk to you,' Mr Hall added.

'Hope she gets the sack!' Annabelle whispered again, and giggled.

Lucy Jane felt uncontrollable panic rush through her and left the caravan in a daze. What had she done wrong? What could it be? Then she thought maybe it was to do with the surprise Mr Savage wanted to talk to her father about when filming was finished.

So she rushed back to the wardrobe caravan and with Thomasina's help changed as quickly as she could.

'You ready?' Mr Hall called as he knocked on the caravan door a few minutes later.

'Yes, I'm coming,' Lucy Jane replied and jumped down the caravan steps and waited anxiously for the director to give his news.

'I'll drive you home, Lucy, while they're setting up the next shot. They won't be ready for at least half an hour,' and he walked towards his car. Lucy Jane followed.

'Listen, Lucy, I have something I want to say to you,'

the director said when they arrived at the farmhouse.

Lucy Jane's heart beat very fast. She was afraid.

'Lucy,' he said quietly, his hand still resting on the wheel. 'You are doing very well in the film, but I think it's best if you don't come to see the rushes any more.'

Lucy Jane lowered her head and looked at her hands. She didn't speak. She hoped he wouldn't say anything worse.

'It's different for the other actors,' Mr Hall continued. 'They've done lots of television and they're used to watching themselves on the screen.'

'What about Andy?' Lucy Jane piped in.

'Yes, he's used to it, too,' Mr Hall said. 'Lucy, you're doing so well. I'm really pleased with you. What you are doing is just what I want. It would be silly to spoil it by your getting upset each day.'

'Are you really pleased with me?' Lucy Jane asked.

'Yes, Lucy, something about you is very special, quite different from the other children.' And he wanted to add that her acting was so real that it had made him both laugh and cry. But he thought it was better for Lucy Jane that she didn't hear such compliments.

Then Mr Hall kissed her on the head and helped her out of the car, chatting about everything except the film as they waited for Mrs Tamm to come and answer the door.

When Lucy Jane walked into the house her granny was waiting in the hall for her.

'Hello, dearie, you must be tired? Would you like some hot milk and biscuits?' she said as Lucy Jane laid her script on the hall table. Lucy Jane nodded eagerly. 'Come on then, to bed, to bed, my sleepy head,' she added and ushered Lucy Jane up to the bathroom to have a lovely hot bath while she went downstairs and

117

prepared the milk and honey.

When Lucy Jane had finished her milk and biscuits and she had cleaned her teeth, Mrs Mackenzie kissed her warmly and said, 'Off to sleep quickly, darling. I have a surprise for you and if you stay up any later you'll spoil it.'

'Another surprise,' Lucy Jane thought and she snuggled down to sleep without being given a chance to find out what the second surprise of the day was to be.

12

The Best Thing of All

The next morning, despite the promise of two surprises, Lucy Jane woke much later than usual. To her amazement, when she opened her eyes, her mother was leaning over the bed looking at her.

'Mummy!' she shrieked with happiness. 'When did you arrive?'

'We drove up through the night,' Mrs Tadworth said, as she hugged her daughter.

'Where's Jeremy?' Lucy Jane asked. At that moment Jeremy came toddling into the room. Lucy Jane bounced out of bed and ran over to him and picked him up.

'How are you, Pickle?' she asked. 'Have you been naughty?'

Jeremy didn't answer, but looked at her, and pointed to Lucy Jane.

'Me?' Lucy Jane smiled. 'Yes, I've been very naughty,

but I've been having an adventure too. You must come and see me. I'm an actress now.'

Jeremy put his chin down on to his chest and looked up at her with his big round eyes. A funny look that made Lucy Jane want to laugh.

'You are a silly,' she said and gave him a squeeze, so happy to see him again.

It was wonderful for Lucy Jane to be with her mother and father. After all the exchanging of news it was decided that her parents would visit her on the set the next time she filmed, and so a few days later the whole family came to the castle. As soon as they arrived Mr Hall took Mr Tadworth to one side and said, 'I'd like to talk to you seriously about your daughter when I've more time once we get back to London.' He smiled at Lucy Jane's father.

'How has she been?' Mr Tadworth asked, worried that there had been some problem that he hadn't been told about.

'Pretty good on the whole,' the director replied. 'She's done a few silly things, but as far as her performance goes it's been splendid. Just perfect.'

Mr Tadworth was relieved.

'But it's important that we discuss her future properly when the filming is over,' Mr Hall said and left Mr Tadworth happy with the news his daughter was doing well.

The filming passed comparatively uneventfully, with all the children acting amicably together, and Lucy Jane doing her best to be friends with Annabelle, who made a point of trying to be unkind to her. But to everyone else Lucy Jane was their mascot.

At lunchtime Lucy Jane usually stayed in the caravan with Miss Notts and learnt her lines while the others went to rushes, and from time to time Angela would come to visit the set. But there were no more practical jokes and the two girls always behaved impeccably.

Most of Lucy Jane's scenes were with Andy, and Sarah Woods whom she liked very much. Although Lucy Jane's part was not very long the scenes were important and dramatic and were bound to make a great impression when the television film was shown to the public. As Lucy Jane had acted so well everyone knew her performance could turn her into a star.

On the days Lucy Jane was not filming there were family picnics and cart rides, walks and outings on the river. Mr Tadworth mended all the bicycles so that the Tadworth family could ride about the countryside. Jeremy was strapped in a special little seat on the back of Mr Tadworth's bike, and Lucy Jane and her mother filled their bicycle baskets with apples and cheese, and cool drinks wrapped in a clean tea towel to refresh everyone when they stopped.

The summer was still fine and the days long and warm. In the evening the family sat on the verandah and did puzzles and played 'Sorry' after Jeremy had gone to bed.

When finally the filming was finished Lucy Jane decided it was quite one of the most wonderful summer holidays she had ever spent. She had a new interest in life now. Acting. It was exciting pretending to be someone else. Crying, being angry, or laughing because the script told you to and because, in a sense, you had become the person you were pretending to be.

As Lucy Jane helped pack her case to go home and she put her script into her Snoopy lunch box for the last time, she had to fight back the tears. It was not just because the film was over, but also because she was leaving her granny, Tammy, her favourite chocolate smartie cake and the koala bear and her new friend Angela.

'Goodbye, Granny,' Lucy Jane said, still trying to control the tears. She flung her arms round her granny's neck as her grandmother kissed her goodbye.

'Goodbye, dearie, I'll be down to see you in London quicker than you think.'

'I hope so, Granny,' Lucy Jane sobbed and gave her

grandmother an even bigger squeeze.

When they had returned to London, Mr Savage telephoned Mr Tadworth and asked if they could meet and talk about the 'surprise' he had mentioned to Lucy Jane in Scotland.

'John Hall and I would like to put Lucy Jane under contract and star her in the television sequel to *The Russell Adventure*. It's the best part,' Mr Savage insisted. 'The Adventure is only a small bite of the cherry. Although she should make her mark in this TV film, the next one will make her into a big star.' He paused again. 'Think about it,' he added. 'Don't forget she has an unusual and very special quality. There are not many children with her natural ability to make you love and care about her all in one.'

Mr Tadworth was completely taken aback by the whole proposition, and relieved that Mr Savage didn't need an answer right away.

After dinner that evening, when Lucy Jane had gone to bed, Mr Tadworth said to his wife, 'You know I met the film producer Marty Savage today. Well, he wants to contract Lucy Jane to star in their next television film.'

'Contract?' Mrs Tadworth repeated, amazed.

'Yes, they think she might make quite a hit in this and they want her to star in their sequel.'

Mrs Tadworth slowly shook her head. She was amazed that she had so little difficulty in thinking. 'No, I don't think it's a good idea. It would spoil her childhood, her schooling and change her life completely.'

'I know what you're thinking,' her husband puffed on his pipe, still not convinced. 'I suppose it doesn't matter in the school holidays,' he said, 'but, yes,' he nodded again, 'I suppose we need to give this more thought.'

So Mr and Mrs Tadworth discussed the proposition for some time: agreeing that it was a too big a chance for Lucy Jane to miss and they should accept, then minutes later deciding against acceptance.

In the end they both decided that they had to refuse. They knew that as far as Lucy Jane was concerned, it was best for her to finish her schooling and live like a normal child.

Lucy Jane knew nothing of this and lay in bed thinking about when the film would be shown on television.

Although Lucy Jane had experienced profound delight in the special atmosphere of the television set and had enjoyed all the fuss and spoiling that went with it almost as much as she had enjoyed being in the ballet, her life was now back to normal and she quickly found herself in the routine of school work, ballet lessons and homework.

One day at breaktime her best friend Julie, who had given her the plastic purse she had taken on holiday to Scotland, said, 'Lucy, Mummy showed me a picture in the newspaper today, of someone who looks just like you in a television programme called *The Russell Adventure*.'

Lucy Jane blushed. Since she had been back at school she had not mentioned to a soul that she had made a television film in the summer holidays as her parents had asked her not to. They felt it would make Lucy Jane feel different from the other children and they might be jealous or she might get teased.

But now when Lucy Jane's best friend asked her if she was in the television show, she felt embarrassed that she hadn't said a word about her amazing holiday except that she had made two new friends, Angela and Andy.

'I'll tell you all about it when you come to tea,' Lucy Jane said to Julie reassuringly. Then during the rest of the break the two girls danced about and practised the steps they had learnt in their ballet lesson.

The Russell Adventure was to be presented as a Christmas Television Special on Boxing Day. The week before Christmas there was a great deal of publicity and Lucy Jane's photograph was in the newspaper almost every day.

The night before the television film was to be shown, Lucy Jane was so excited she could hardly sleep. As she tossed and turned in her pretty peach and white bedroom, she found herself reliving all her summer adventures. In the end she decided to creep downstairs and see her parents.

'Mummy?' she said quietly as she gently pushed open the sitting room door. Her parents were surprised to see her out of bed.

'Lucy, darling, what's the matter? You should be asleep,' her mother said.

Before her mother had time to say more, Lucy Jane asked, 'Mummy, do you think people will think I'm silly on television tomorrow? Do you think they'll think I'm squeaky?' and she pensively stroked her cat Tilly, worried that the viewers would laugh at her, and waited for her mother to reply.

'Squeaky, darling?' her mother repeated, bewildered.

'You know, like I sounded in the rushes. Squeaky,' Lucy Jane said again.

'Oh, Lucy,' her mother said, taking her daughter on her knee and giving her a squeeze. 'I'm sure they'll think you're lovely, darling. I do,' she said and gave her another hug. 'Really, Lucy, you mustn't worry about that,' she continued as she gently pushed back the hair from Lucy Jane's forehead.

Lucy Jane felt very pleased to be having this night-time cuddle and she wound her arms tighter round her mother's neck, and nestled her nose into her mother's hair.

'Now,' her mother said after a time, 'you must go back to bed,' and she took Lucy Jane by the hand so she could give her father a kiss. 'I love the smell of pipe and jumper,' Lucy Jane said as she sniffed her daddy's jersey when she kissed him goodnight.

As her mother gently caressed her cheek with her hand, Lucy Jane fell into a happy sleep.

The next day the household was in a whirl of excitement. The programme was to be shown that afternoon and Lucy Jane could hardly eat she was so nervous. The thought of millions of people watching her on television made her feel quite sick.

After tea, at which Lucy Jane only nibbled a biscuit, the whole family sat on the sofa together. Jeremy sat on his father's knee and Lucy Jane snuggled between her parents ready to watch *The Russell Adventure*.

Before the programme had even finished the telephone started to ring and never stopped; people ringing to say congratulations, and how good they thought Lucy Jane was.

Lucy Jane was amazed everyone thought she was good, especially as she thought she was awful. And when the next day the producer telephoned and said the critics had thought that the show was excellent and had especially praised Lucy Jane's performance, she could hardly believe it.

'She'll be up for an award, mark my words,' Mr

Savage said happily as he put down the receiver.

Sure enough, two months later Lucy Jane received a letter asking her to go to the B.A.F.T.A. Television Awards at the Dorchester Hotel on March 14, as she had been nominated for an award for 'The Best Newcomer'.

When Mr Savage heard that Lucy Jane had been nominated for an award he was so proud and happy that he had a magnificent white dress sent from America for her. It was ballerina length, just above Lucy Jane's ankles, made of white silk organza taffeta with a full skirt and deep frill at the bottom. The puffed sleeves and round collar were piped with the same pale blue as the wide satin sash. When Lucy Jane tried it on for the first time, she thought it was even more beautiful than the dresses in the *Nutcracker* ballet, and she skipped and twirled about the room.

On the day of the awards, the babysitter arrived at two o'clock to look after Jeremy while Mrs Tadworth and Lucy went to have their hair done. Mr Tadworth came home from work early with a little present for Jeremy, so he wouldn't feel left out.

By six-thirty Mr and Mrs Tadworth, Lucy Jane's granny and Lucy Jane were all standing in the hall, changed and ready to leave for the Dorchester Hotel. They looked a grand sight. Jeremy was very excited at seeing everyone dressed up and being allowed to stay out of bed to watch them leave.

He jumped up and down and said, 'Pwitty, pwitty. Uci wery pwitty.'

'Oh, you are sweet,' Lucy said, hugging her brother. 'Let's see the 'pwesent' dada gave you,' she laughed, and Jeremy showed his sister his splendid blue truck.

'Wery pwitty,' Lucy Jane said, teasing him, and at that moment there was a ring at the bell.

A huge, shiny black car, almost as long as the front of Lucy Jane's house, had arrived to collect them, so with a great deal of fuss and chatter they all bundled into the car and waved goodbye to Jeremy and the babysitter.

When they arrived at the hotel, the chauffeur quickly slid out of the driving seat and sped round the side of the car to open the door for Lucy Jane.

Lucy Jane giggled to herself. 'This is like being a princess,' she thought, as she got out of the car, taking care that her beautiful dress was not crushed.

As she stepped on to the red carpet stretched across the pavement, hoards of photographers gathered round her taking photographs and asking questions. It was so unlike anything that had ever happened to Lucy Jane before that she was not at all sure what she was supposed to do. 'My brain is sticking to the top of my head,' she thought. 'No frogs today.'

Her parents pushed her a little further forward and Lucy Jane smiled, surprised by all the fuss while the photographers and television cameras took her picture.

'Excuse me, Miss Tadworth,' a man with a microphone said as he jostled his way forward. 'We're from ITV Television and would like to ask you a few questions.' Lucy Jane looked up at him.

By now crowds outside the hotel were all pushing and shoving to get a better glimpse of the stars, including Lucy Jane. The pavements were spilling with spectators, photographers and television cameras. So much so that the television crew filming Lucy Jane had to call extra police to hold back the crowds.

Then the television interviewer pushed closer and asked, 'How does it feel to be a child star?'

'A star?' Lucy Jane questioned. 'Or do you mean an actress?' she asked earnestly. 'Or do you mean a child?'

The crowd laughed and jostled to get closer and the interviewer continued, rather taken aback by Lucy Jane's reply.

'Well, how does it feel to be alive? I mean to be here?' he corrected himself, getting quite flustered. 'I mean to be nominated for an award?'

Lucy Jane thought for a moment; she was glad her parents and her granny were close behind her and wondered if they too thought the questions the man was asking her were rather silly.

'It's always better to be alive,' Lucy Jane answered carefully. 'But . . . ' and before she could continue the crowd cheered again.

Then her parents said, 'Excuse me,' and ushered Lucy into the hotel.

Inside the huge hotel ballroom, lit by sparkling chandeliers, there were hundreds of television stars chatting at every table, but Lucy Jane was so overawed that she perched on the edge of her chair looking anxiously at her parents on one side of Mr Savage and John Hall on the other, too nervous to talk.

After dinner the big moment came and the names for each award were read out and the actors and actresses went up to collect their prizes. Lucy Jane became more and more frightened, hoping she wouldn't win an award and have to go up on to the stage in front of so many people.

Suddenly she heard the words, 'And the winner of the last award is a young lady who captured all our hearts when *The Russell Adventure* was shown on BBC on Boxing Day . . . Miss Lucy Jane Tadworth, the winner of the 'Best Newcomer Award' for her performance as Isabella in *The Russell Adventure*.'

Lucy Jane's heart stopped in her chest.

'Me?' she asked her mother, her eyes wide with surprise. Her mother nodded and pushed her forward.

'Me!' she repeated to herself as she struggled between the tables to the stage, the sound of the audience's applause and cheers ringing in her ears.

As she arrived on the platform she looked up and realised she had nearly bumped into the Prince who was presenting the award.

'Oh dear, so sorry,' Lucy Jane said. The Prince laughed and ushered her towards the microphone.

'Would you like to say a few words?' the Master of Ceremonies leant over and asked her.

Lucy Jane looked up at the microphone. It looked so tall and far away.

'Well, will they hear me if I can't reach that?' she said, pointing to the microphone.

'I'm sure they will,' the Prince answered kindly and lifted Lucy Jane up to the microphone so she could be heard.

'Well, I'd like to thank my friend Angela for sharing her part and for cutting her hair, and Granny for inviting me to Rockleigh, and everyone for inviting me here, and Mummy and . . . oh yes, and thank the Prince for giving me the prize.'

Everyone laughed. Then the Prince lowered Lucy Jane to the ground and she curtsied and ran from the stage as quickly as she could.

When she arrived back at the table Mr Savage kissed her and said, 'Well done, Lucy. Well done. Now I've a surprise for you,' and he looked at the table. To Lucy Jane's amazement Angela popped out from under the table and said, 'Hello, Orange Pips!' Lucy Jane was so surprised she nearly dropped her award.

Then Mr Savage put his arm round Angela and announced, 'I knew you'd be pleased. Now I have more news. Angela is having reading lessons and as long as she doesn't cut her hair off again she's going to be the star of our next television adventure.'

Lucy Jane was overjoyed and bounced up and down, hugging Angela and saying, 'Jumping cactus, Ange, now we're both actresses.'

'Yes, Orange Pips,' Angela agreed happily. 'AND,' Angela continued, 'I've got some better news.'

She looked at Mrs Tadworth to see if she was allowed to tell Lucy Jane the 'better news'. 'I'm coming to stay with you for the WHOLE weekend!'

'Oh!' Lucy Jane exclaimed excitedly. 'This is LOVELY!' And with that the two girls linked arms and stood smiling as they were photographed.

As she clutched the award to her chest she looked up at her mother and remembered the ballet. Wonderful Covent Garden! A wistful longing came into her heart. She looked round the room filled with stars. A fantastic evening it had been, but nothing for Lucy Jane was as special as the ballet.

Lucy Jane's mother stroked her hair and said, 'We're so proud of you, Lucy,' and Lucy Jane felt a little lump in her throat. She looked down at the award in her hands and whispered to the frog in her head, 'This is what you get if you don't mind being second choice.'

*Also by Susan Hampshire
and available from Mammoth*

LUCY JANE
AT THE
BALLET

When Lucy Jane's mother has to go into
hospital, Lucy Jane is sent to stay with her Aunt
Sarah. She is most reluctant to go, she wants to
stay at home with her father and her cat, Tilly.

But Lucy Jane doesn't realise what surprises lie
in store for her, for Aunt Sarah is wardrobe
mistress at the Theatre Royal, Covent Garden
and Lucy Jane is swiftly drawn into the life of a
ballet company.

She meets everyone; the stage doorkeeper and
his little dog, the dressers, the electricians, the
stage-hands, the choreographer, the Company
Manager but most important of all, Tatiana
Marova, the prima ballerina, who takes her
under her wing.

The story of Lucy Jane's change of heart, and
her unexpected involvement in the special Royal
Gala Performance of *The Nutcracker* is an
exciting one, and Vanessa Julian-Ottie's
illustrations, drawn from life, add to the magic
of the setting.

Berlie Doherty
TILLY MINT TALES

I don't know if you've ever met Tilly Mint. She's about as old as you, I should think.

When Tilly's mum goes out to work, Mrs Hardcastle from up the street pops in to look after her. She's very old. Very old. She once told Tilly that she was the oldest woman in the world.

Now, there are two special things about Mrs Hardcastle. The first thing is, she's always dropping off to sleep. And the second special thing is that when she does, something magic happens to Tilly Mint. She visits the island of dreams, she learns not to be afraid, not of lions or anything, and she rides on the owl's back to the stars that sing...

Berlie Doherty's first book for younger children shows her perfection as a storyteller and her gift for celebrating all living things.

Berlie Doherty

TILLY MINT AND THE DODO

'I was trying to hug you,' said Tilly, 'because I'm
so happy to see you.'

The Dodo clucked deep in her throat, pleased,
looking a bit pink for a bird. 'People don't usually
hug dodos, Tilly,' she said shyly. 'They hunt us,
and they shoot us. Or they stuff us. They eat us,
usually. But they never hug us. Never.'

'They hunt you, Dodo? Why? Why would they
do that?'

'I don't know,' said Dodo sadly. 'They don't
really seem to like us very much...'

And so begins Tilly's friendship with the very last
Dodo on earth, and her adventures in the land of
yesterday to save her new friend from extinction.
Helped by the magic of her old friend, Mrs
Hardcastle, she enables Dodo to escape from the
hunters, but they face an even more terrifying
enemy in the pirates...

Tilly Mint and the Dodo is a brilliant and moving
exploration of the conservation issue by award-
winning author Berlie Doherty and is beautifully
illustrated by Janna Doherty.